Holly Blue

Cyprus born Yianoulla Nicola came to England as a young child. Since her school years she has always wanted to write. Now her children have flown the nest she has enjoyed putting her passion to paper.

Holly Blue is her first novel.

Holly Blue
by Yianoulla Nicola

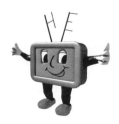

published by HandE Publishers Ltd

First published in the United Kingdom in 2007
By HandE Publishers Ltd
Epping Film Studios, Brickfield Business
Centre, Thornwood High Road,
Epping, Essex CM16 6TH
www.handepublishers.co.uk

A CIP catalogue record for this book is available from
The British Library

IBSN - 0-9548518-3-8
IBSN - 978-0-9548518-3-5

Edited by Emma Batrick
Cover design by Creation Studio
Type set by Lynn Jones
First printed and bound in 2007 by
Kowa Stationery Ltd, 16-18 Hing Yip St,
Kwun Tong,Kowloon,HK

Dedication

To my Yia 'Ya Sofia

A Funeral...1985.

It was the most beautiful day, no different from any other beautiful day in August. I looked up but I had never seen it before, not like this, the sky was powder blue.

'As blue as his eyes,' I heard myself whisper.

I wondered how far up it all went, how deep? If I reached hard enough could I touch that one little cloud up there all alone? I was as invisible as a ghost was. A part of me had stopped living the day he died, a piece was missing.

'Sofia?' I heard Christina say. 'Sofia?'

Just as I was about to touch my cloud in the sky, her voice pulled me back, back to where I didn't want to be. I turned to look at her and for a moment forgot where I was and why; for that single moment I didn't have to face this reality - because my reality was somewhere else.

'It's your turn Sofia,' she said, her voice sounding cheerless and empty as she handed me a white rose.

I reached out to take it from her and the dazzling sun shone upon the crystal butterfly hanging from my bracelet, making it sparkle like a rare diamond, and that's when I saw its' wings flicker as it came back to life.

I put the rose up to my face but even its velvety petals seemed to turn poignant to my touch.

Yes, it was my turn, I thought and I closed my eyes......

Winter, November 1976, England.

Chapter One

'Sofia, are you up? You must get ready for school. Christina! Irini! You're going to be late!' It was so cold outside and I didn't want to get up. My sisters were opening and closing doors, running around the house trying to get ready, but I didn't want to go. I would much rather have stayed at home with mama and my baby sister Elizabeth.

'Sofia!' Mama said, opening my bedroom door. 'Sofia, come on my sweet girl.' She continued.

The snow had not stopped falling all night, quite unusual for this time of the year. November wasn't normally bitterly cold and snow usually came at Christmas, yet although it would be Christmas soon, the winter had arrived first. I hated this season - I hated the winter. The heavily fringed velvet curtains in my room would soon be drawn open, unveiling the cold darkened morning, and as she sat down beside me, she began stroking my hair, she knew me well enough to know I didn't want to go to school. I pulled the crumpled satin blanket over my head but I could still feel her tender and loving touch.

Elena Constantine, my mama, was a kind, gentle woman, and extremely beautiful. She first met my papa at school when she was just nine years old and he was twelve. He always boasted they had fallen in love at first sight, and that from the moment he saw her, he knew, that one day, he would make her his wife. But what did mama know about love? What did any young Greek girl know about true love? If you were fortunate enough to come from a good family where your father and his father, and his father before him, had wealth in any shape, there would be a good chance you would marry a 'prince', a Greek 'prince' of course! You would be expected to have lots of beautiful babies and live happily ever after. And even though my mama loved my papa very much all that really mattered was that she was his 'princess' and he was her 'prince'!

2

Winter, November 1976, England.

'Sofia'. She gently tugged, but I would not be going to school and that was that! 'I'll draw the curtains Miss Sofia,' Blasted Mrs Bradshaw on entering my room.

Why? I thought. Does nobody understand me? Is everybody deaf?

'Come, I'll lay out your clothes for you,' she continued, pretending not to notice me still lying in my warm bed.

She was a stubborn woman, Georgina Bradshaw, tight lipped one could say. Employed as house keeper a week before Christmas day when my sister Elizabeth was born. It wasn't mama's intention to hire on such impulse but considering the circumstances due to a new arrival on top of the festive season it felt right.

Her and her husband Ernest Bradshaw, our butler, lived with us at Holly Blue. Only a weak man such as Mr Bradshaw could be woven into her web, she knew how to get her own way around with him, and I was to be no exception. So knowing I was to do as I was told, I washed, got dressed and was ready as ordered.

'Have a good day my little darlings. Mr Bradshaw is outside, and it's quite freezing, lets not keep him waiting.' Said my mama, kissing the three of us goodbye.

We stepped out to the bitter cold and into a warmed Bentley; papa's other 'baby'. Christina stared excitedly at the frozen garden, Irini took out a paperback book from her bag and I sat staring back in silence as the car pulled away.

Holly Blue... What a house! It stood so grand in all its splendour, almost becoming invisible where the snow had camouflaged it into the surrounding white scenery, every tree and every branch draped, creating small white puffballs of the once green bushes and hedgerows.

'Look! Sofia! Look!' Christina shrieked, pressing her nose against the frosty window with excitement. 'Look at the rabbits!'

Her sudden enthusiasm pulled me away.

Christina shrieked again!

They were leaping like ballerinas as they danced in the snow, their furry white costumes keeping them warm. Irini didn't care, she was reading her book, one of many romantic novels she owned and no amount of snow or dancing rabbits would spoil the world she'd disappeared into. She turned the page, looked over at us for just one

3

Winter, November 1976, England.

second, looked out of the window and then returned to her world.

'Can you see them Sofia? Can you?' Christina asked.

'Yes, yes!' I replied, our cheeks almost touching and my nose mirroring hers as I pressed my face against the window too.

Then taking my own enthusiasm away from the ballerinas for a moment, I looked at Christina, for her joy was not to be missed, she was a great character, so full of essence! Only when the dancing bunnies were out of sight did she take her face away from the frosty window. With the thirty minute drive to school always seeming much longer on these cold winter mornings, I cuddled up to her, for too soon would we be parting - she was two years younger than me and two classes below. We held each other lovingly, admiring this winter picture postcard landscape. The snow that had settled over the fields and on the rooftop of Guilbey Farm, next door, resembling soft icing sugar ready to be turned into marvellous meringues.

We just sat, as we often did, in silence as Mr Bradshaw drove with great caution around the frozen bendy lanes deep into the forest; its tyre marks being the only thing spoiling this perfect scene and leaving behind the only evidence of us having been there. However, my perfect picture postcard immediately turned dull as I noticed a baby rabbit lying still by the road side, and I wondered if his mama was looking for him and how sad she would be when she eventually found his frozen and lifeless little body. It saddened me to think that she would never see him again, not be able to love or play with her cherished young.

I snuggled up to Christina and closed my eyes for the rest of the journey.

As soon as the car approached the main entrance of Wilbury Manor School, Mr Bradshaw found a safe place to park and got out to open the car door. I stepped out carefully onto the slush covered pavement, first taking hold of Christina's arm then Irini's, and we began walking briskly towards the great iron gates, heading for the tiny playground. I kissed them both and we parted, each of us heading in a different direction to our classrooms. Yet that was never enough for me and I turned to catch one last glimpse of them, quickly calling out for one more goodbye, but they couldn't hear me because of the freezing wind which had now picked up speed, it was so loud - howling like a wolf in the night.

'*Goodbye Christina, goodbye Irini,*' I sighed to myself, running against the wind as I held tightly on to my hat with one hand and my skirt with the other. Eventually, I came to the green door that led to a long, narrow corridor, and even though it was quite heavy, I managed to pull it open letting it slam shut behind me. Right away it hit me the smell of school, the smell of coats and plimsolls, pencils and powder paints, the smell of which I both liked and loathed. With my pace having now almost come to a halt, I stopped to take a breather as I began my eager search for her, and as I glanced up at the beautifully decorated wall that was camouflaged in an array of dazzling butterflies, she was there... '*The Holly Blue, By Sofia Constantine*', I read it out aloud, admiring my masterpiece.

All of a sudden, I had a feeling someone was standing behind me. I swung around and there he was; oh my God, it was him - it was Jonathan Guilbey!

'Hello,' I said, clumsily dropping my book bag, spilling its contents all over the floor.

Hello,' he said with a grin. 'Do you need any help?'

'No thanks,' I replied, gathering them up as quickly as I could, trying to spare myself more embarrassment.

Nevertheless he bent down to help me, and my only thought was to get up and run!

It was 1964 and I was just two years old when we first met. I still get flash backs of the day mama took us to see our new house in Essex. Heavily pregnant with Christina, she'd decided to take us out for the day hoping it might bring on the birth. Mama had a tendency of always getting her dates wrong. She'd got them wrong first with Irini and then eighteen months later with me, so why should it have been any different with Christina? The long drive through London was painfully hot on this scolding July afternoon and at one point mama had to stop the car and get out for some fresh air.

'Is everything okay?' Asked a man, who'd pulled up alongside us thinking Elena, my mama, was in trouble or maybe lost.

'We are heading for a place near Guilbey Farm, do you know it?'

Winter, November 1976, England.

'Yes of course we're going that way too,' he smiled, 'I'm Henry Guilbey,' he introduced himself shaking Elena's hand. 'And this is my good wife Margaret. We live at Guilbey Farm,' he said, cocking his cap.

'Hello,' she greeted his kindness, 'I am Elena and these are my two girls, Irini and Sofia.'

'It seems we have a little something in common,' Margaret exclaimed rubbing her pregnant bump.

'Well it does seem we have,' Elena agreed, patting her tummy. 'It's very kind of you to stop.'

'Where near Guilbey Farm are you going to?' Asked Henry.

'A place called 'Holly Blue Lane'; we are off to see our new home.'

'Well I'll be damned,' laughed Henry. 'Not only are we at your service, but we're your new neighbours too!' He jumped back into his car. 'Follow us!' He called.

The short drive through the forest that led Elena to Guilbey Farm was also to lead to her new life. As she turned into the narrow, bendy lane, it suddenly came into view, *Holly Blue House.*

'There it is,' Margaret informed her, pointing up at the house. 'There's your beautiful new home.' She then turned and said, 'why not come to the farm for a cup of tea first? You must be thirsty, and you can meet Grandma Guilbey and Jonathan.'

'Thank you, you're so kind, only if you're sure it's okay Mrs Guilbey? We don't want to...'

'Please, call me Margaret, and yes I am sure,' she interrupted as mama very proudly excused us from being her guest. Mama hated being a burden to anyone.

'It is very kind thank you, please call me Elena.' She agreed.

That's when I met their son Jonathan Guilbey for the first time; he was playing on the kitchen floor with his toy soldiers busily lining them up as they prepared for battle.

*   *   *   *   *   *   *   *   *

'May, wait!' I called to her to stop. 'Let's sit together.'

I took hold of her arm, quickly leading her to our classroom, and before we'd even sat down, we started to giggle. May had that affect on me, and I on her, which was why Miss Harris, our form teacher, forbade us from sitting together. However, it was the beginning of the week, Monday, 5th November 1976 - Guy Fawkes Day and new weeks began with new promises.

'Good morning, class,' Miss Harris said, welcoming us all back from the weekend; her face was stern and her voice high pitched.

'Good morning Miss Harris.' We replied all together in an un-orderly manner, pushing back our chairs as we rose to our feet.

She tilted her head forward, and with a look of disturbance asked if we could '*sit down*'. Then one by one she called out our names as she took the register:

'Paris Bandelli.'

'Here Miss Harris.'

'Keith Barton.'

'Here Miss Harris.'

'Martin Berry.'

'Here Miss Harris.'

'Sofia Constantine... Sofia Constantine...' she repeated in her piercing, high pitch...'Sofia Constantine,' she said, higher still.

'Sofia,' whispered May, giving me a nudge, knowing too well the high pitch may decrease as soon as I answer. 'Sofia,' whispered May, giving me a nudge.

'Sorry Miss...Yes Miss. I mean here Miss Harris,' I stammered.

When Miss Harris had finished taking the register and her high pitch echo had subsided, she asked us to start making our way to the main hall, which lay in a smaller building across from the tiny playground. With its doors already open, we entered in silence. It was fairly small compared to other school halls, but I loved everything about it, especially its stained glass windows, which we were told St Andrew's, the Catholic Church next door had kindly donated when the school was first built. They were astonishingly beautiful and dominated the walls with their vibrant colours. We sat cross-legged on the freshly polished floor, and right away I began desperately searching for Christina and Irini...'*Where are my sisters?*' I thought.

I was such a fragile, delicate child - a child with a free spirit who wanted to fly but was too scared for fear of where my journey might take me and the disappointment I would face if I failed.

Winter, November 1976, England.

With another nudge from May, I was made aware of Jonathan Guilbey's entrance to the hall. Papa said we weren't to talk to, or look at boys, so I tried not to look his way and carried on my search for my sisters, but as I turned towards his stare, our eyes met, he smiled at me, and I blushed. May passed me the hymn book and we started to sing.

May and I had become inseparable from the very first day we met, September 7th 1965, we were only three years old. We'd sat next to one another during our first art lesson. Our art teacher, Miss Carter, who was still at the school, had to tie May's hair back because Martin Berry had pulled it loose and had snapped her flowery hair band in the process. I still remember her crying – it seemed like she cried all day, so making her my most important responsibility, I didn't leave her side. Eleven years had past since that day and now May and I were truly convinced we were telepathic; soul mates!

We turned the page as another hymn began and by now the snow had started to fall, I could hear the sound of the echoing wind as it gracefully took the white essence round and round, up and down. Together they danced in harmony becoming one for they knew they looked beautiful and they demanded an audience, *'The rabbits with their furry white costumes would not be left to dance alone,'* I sighed.

A week later, 1976 England.

Chapter Two

The Sunday morning after Guy Fawkes was still very bitter and cold, but at last the snow had now melted, and even though we hadn't celebrated on the actual day, we were promised a fireworks party at grandma's, my *yia'ya* Athena's house.

I sat in my bedroom waiting for papa to return home so that we could leave, but he'd become quite an expert at always being late.

'Mr Bradshaw, do you have the time please?' I heard mama ask as they passed one another in the hallway.

'Its twenty past nine Miss Elena, is everything alright?'

'Yes. Well no,' she replied, trying to stay composed, but there was agitation in her voice. 'Harry's late and we're supposed to be leaving soon.'

'Can I do anything to help?'

'Thank you Mr Bradshaw, I wish there was. We'll wait 'til half past, he's probably on his way home,' she answered, making her way downstairs.

'Hello Maritsa, we're running a little late darling, so you best make your way to church and we'll meet you there.' I could hear her informing Auntie Maritsa from the telephone downstairs. 'Harry is...' She announced; 'HERE! Maritsa we're on our way,' she said, hanging up the receiver hearing papa parking up in front of the house. 'Girls!' She called for us to come downstairs. 'Papa is here let's go, put your coats on. Let's go!'

It was Sunday - church day - and there shouldn't have been an uncomfortable silence in the car, but there was. We knew all was not well between our parents and we dared not misbehave, so Irini took out a book from her bag while Christina and I exchanged whispers about whether George and Anthony Parras would be gracing us with their presence today. I hated it when our parents didn't speak to one another, it created an awkward atmosphere, dampening the mood and

A week later, 1976 England.

putting us on edge, not that we'd ever witnessed any violence, just deep mood swings from mama resulting in Christina, Irini and I sitting in the back almost becoming invisible and hoping it wouldn't take too long for papa to lift mama's frame of mind with one of his flirtatious smiles, because as angry as she was with him, his smile always seemed to do the trick.

However, as St Mary's came into view I secretly imagined that perhaps she also had something to do with it; maybe she brought back happy memories of their wedding day. Memories had a funny way of doing that, and St Mary's had plenty of them, from weddings to christenings and even sad funerals, whatever the occasion she was always there playing hostess. Though I knew going to church served another purpose too, it was the perfect meeting place for a single Greek 'princess' to meet a future husband, and if you were to marry a nice Greek 'prince' then you would have to attend church on Sundays. Therefore, there we were, wearing our best frocks and putting on our brightest smiles!

Upon entering the tranquil building the strong smell of burning dried olive leaves smouldering in their silver incense burners was the first thing to attack my senses. It was a smell we'd become quite accustomed to over the years, coming home from school and having either mama or *yia'ya* Athena follow us around the house holding a burner over our heads - blessing us and warding off bad luck.

I lit a candle, which I placed into the beautifully carved wooden sand-filled tray before kissing every Icon in sight - and there were plenty of them. There were Icons on walls in the front, on the sides and at the back; they looked at us from everywhere! Then as if by chance I found a small space to squeeze into on a bench, though if asked I would have happily given it up to a little old Greek lady who needed it more than I did. Mama sat holding baby Elizabeth near the front with my *yia'ya* and her two sisters, Stella and Maritsa. They always got to church as early as possible, sitting near the front to get the best view.

'*Kali'mera*, Mrs Michalli. What a wonderful morning,' the priest said, taking hold of *yia'ya's* hand, welcoming her as she was about to sit down.

'*Kali'mera* Reverend, it is a lovely morning today,' she said very

10

A week later, 1976 England.

earnestly, bending down to kiss his hand - she took going to church very seriously.

Christina, Irini and papa stood near the back, happy to be surrounded by the other worshippers who were keeping them warm with the heat coming from the candles they were holding. I watched as they stood patiently listening to the priest as he spoke about good and bad, right and wrong, of lives past and present, and when he eventually finished his sermon, I joined in with the rest of the congregation as he led the reciting of a prayer from the Holy Bible. More interested in glancing up at the massive chandelier hanging from the high ceiling, I was mumbling more than reciting. As my eyes wandered I suddenly caught sight of George Parras sitting with his brother Anthony and our eyes met. I shied away from his stare, reminding myself of a certain cold morning in the school hall, and for a moment I began daydreaming about Jonathan Guilbey. Becoming aware that my daydream was turning my prayer into a mumble, I looked down and continued, hoping nobody had noticed. When the prayer had finally finished, I started making my way out into the front garden where I would be meeting and greeting old friends and distant relatives.

'Sofia, come here my sweet girl,' said *yia'ya* Athena, inviting me into the warmth of her embrace. Quickly taking her up on her offer, I wrapped my arms around her, my hold gradually turning into a squeeze, and all at once I smelt her rose scented perfume. It was so comforting and so familiar; I would have stayed there forever if I could. 'We won't be too long now,' she smiled down stroking my long hair. 'I think we've just about said hello to everyone,' she comforted me. 'And did I see a certain young man at church today?' She asked.

I looked up at her and thought how much I absolutely loved and adored her.

'Yes!' I replied, with an enthusiastic response. 'Yes, George is here. Do you think he's handsome *yia'ya?*'

'Oh yes! Very!' She agreed with a smile.

Then catching mama's attention, she waved at her as if to say, '*let's go*'. With that, we swiftly said our goodbyes and headed for the cemetery where *bapou* Christos had been buried five years after a tragic accident, November 12th 1971 to be exact. Visits to my *bapou* Christos's grave were no easier now than when he first passed away.

11

A week later, 1976 England.

Grandpa's was the first funeral I had the misfortune to attend, quickly realizing that death and funerals were not taken lightly by Greeks. I was sure my *yia'ya* thought the rest of the world had stopped living the day he died, and as a result, resolved to a life on valium.

I watched with an inner stillness, as she gently placed the lovely bouquet of flowers that she'd grown in her greenhouse, into a large vase. I wasn't sure what to do, I so wanted to comfort her, but instead I just stood taking it all in. The lessons of life were sometimes so hard, even for someone as young as me, and as my family took their time grooming the marble headstone and arranging the beautiful flowers, it suddenly began to rain. It may have been *bapou* saying, *'thank you for coming,'* his way of sending us home, but whatever it was, our visit was now over and we began to make our way to *yia'ya* Athena's house.

Naturally, my *yia'ya* would have everything under control, but cooking for the whole family was no easy task. Although I couldn't think of anything she loved more than to have us all around her – doing what she did best; *'fuss'*. Everybody helped with the cooking, though today there would be no need for fine china, or crystal glasses, no hurry to polish the best silver cutlery, today we would be treated to a casual affair! And being that we were the first to arrive, Christina had given herself the all important role of hostess, which she did with pride. Her job was to welcome everybody with a kiss on the cheek, take their hats and coats and guide them into the kitchen.

'This looks fantastic *yia'ya*,' said Uncle Mike, referring to what seemed like one million platters that sat unspoilt on the pine *Lefka'ridiko* lace covered table.

He clicked away with his camera.

'Where's Harry? Does he need more help with the bonfire?' He continued, from behind the lens.

'Hello Mike!' Called papa. 'You should stop taking photos of the food, and take some of your lovely wife,' he laughed at him with open arms. Then turning to Aunt Demi he gave her a flirtatious smile and said, 'hello gorgeous, you're looking as lovely as ever.'

'Oh stop it Harry,' she replied approvingly kissing him on the cheek. 'Stop encouraging him,' she continued. 'Mr Vasiliou - *photographer of the year* - has taken enough of me to last a life time.' She

A week later, 1976 England.

then turned to *yia'ya* trying to ignore papa's presence, 'you've done us proud. It does look fantastic.'

'Thank you Demi,' *yia'ya* smiled, accepting her compliments with pride, 'Now come everyone - let's eat!' She called to us, waving her arms towards the food.

In no time, glasses were filled to the brim and everyone cheered *'ce'yiamas'*! And as all the adults continued to raise their glasses, drinking to good health, Christina, Irini and I sat together by the small bay window in the dining room facing the back garden. From there we could see the bonfire papa and Uncle Mike had erected earlier that day and on top sat our very own Guy Fawkes awaiting his gruesome fate.

Mrs Bradshaw had helped us clear out our wardrobes earlier that week, giving everything that was too small to the charity shop in the village near where we lived, but she had made sure to keep back some items for us to dress him with, though papa never let us go out like other children asking: '*A penny for the Guy.*'

When everyone had finished eating and my Aunties Stella and Maritsa had finally stopped asking poor *yia'ya* for the names of every herb and spice that she'd put into some of the dishes - that were now not so unspoilt - we could clear up and go outside. All the women and girls gathered into the small kitchen to lend a hand; resembling factory workers. We stood in a row armed with our tea towels for the drying. Auntie Maritsa did the washing up, while mama helped *yia'ya* put everything away. This was how it had always been done from the time I could remember, the women and girls in the kitchen - a place where the men and boys banned themselves from. This was *'women's* work' the men would say as they sat in the room at the front of the house smoking and drinking Cypriot coffee.

Only when the dishes were washed and cleared away would we be ready to make our way down the slippery steps into the back garden to join the men who had congregated there already.

My Auntie Stella always enthusiastically led the way, because apart from being well persevered with her slender physique and ample bosom, which had not changed from when she was a young girl, she was still as lively and as zany as ever. She was never able to be away from her beloved husband Uncle Nick for too long, a charmingly

13

A week later, 1976 England.

British, yet, very Greek man who was just as crazy as her. She would run towards him as if it were their first ever encounter.

Uncle Nick constantly smelt of fish and chips, something we'd all become accustomed to as he ran his own fish 'n' chip shop in the town centre where they lived. He reminded us of Father Christmas with his stocky build and bushy pure white moustache, which always tickled whenever he gave us a kiss. He and Auntie Stella had two sons, my cousins Fivo and Christos.

Auntie Maritsa on the other hand, was more subdued. Not as crazy and less slender, a little more like *yia'ya* Athena, mirroring her in every way - two-piece suits, pearls and a passion for gardening. She had fulfilled *yia'ya's* own ambition of becoming a school teacher. She was here with her husband, George Georgiou: he was an accountant, though I wasn't too sure what that was exactly, but he always looked serious, spoke with a posh English accent and wore nothing but dark suits. They had two daughters, my cousins Helen and little Anna, and a son, my lovely cousin Kiri.

Uncle Mike, mama's cousin, had arrived with his fashion designer wife, Dimitra, the very trendy and extremely lovely Aunt Demi as we called her. She always had plenty of time for us - dressing up, exchanging fashion tips and discreetly talking with us about boys. Aunt Demi and Uncle Mike were unable to have children of their own, so to make up for their dreadful loss, they put it upon themselves to become the proud godparents of every child that was born into the family. And of course, last but not at all least, there was the hostess of the night, my *yia'ya* Athena.

With so many of us walking to the bottom of this wet and slimy garden and we had to be very careful. Christina, Irini and I took hold of *yia'ya* Athena and gently guided her over the no longer green but muddy golden-yellow ground, only safely getting there with light that was reflecting down upon us from the colourful lanterns she'd hung on the trees. All the way, she kept telling us how she'd hung them there because she couldn't stand seeing the trees so bare now that they were not bursting with ripened delicious apples and pears. But even though *yia'ya's* garden was not packed with fantastic fruits and flowers, there was still a charming quaintness about it; its cobbled pathway that led to her secret garden where figurines stood in

14

A week later, 1976 England.

between rockeries and its two wooden benches inscribed with *yia'ya* and *bapou's* names sat side by side near the koi carp filled pond. Many a time we would come to visit on a Friday only to find her sitting out here reminiscing on times gone by.

'Come on everybody, say cheese!' Called Uncle Mike from behind his lens again. But instead we shouted: '*Haloumi*!' And as we all laughed - he clicked! Finally he put the thing down, lit a fire lighter and in a flash there was a whoosh and the huge bonfire was ablaze. Its bright golden flames climbed up and up, higher and higher until they reached our Guy, and with another wave of his wand our sparklers were alive! Joyfully whooshing our arms around in the air, we skipped as the burning cartwheels joined in with us.

Then suddenly, BANG! The rockets lit up the night sky turning it into day, again and again... BANG! BANG! We began screaming with elation; even the adults seemed to have forgotten their cares.

There was definitely something so special about being at my *yia'ya's* house. It always brought out the best in everyone and I truly believed she was the Christmas fairy that sat at the top of our tree, listening to all our wishes and dreams, sprinkling her magic dust and making miracles come true. This tiny house with its tiny rooms was not a large Manor, nor was it full of priceless arts. There were no grand hallways with chandeliers sparkling at night, but it was a castle in its own right, with 'maidens' and 'lords,' 'princes' and 'princesses', even 'dragons' and 'heroes' - and of course, our very own Christmas fairy that sat at the top of the tree.

* * * * * * * * *

Waking up early the next morning was very unusual for me, but as I gathered my thoughts of last night, I washed, got dressed and went down for breakfast without a fuss. Mrs Bradshaw must have thought it was Christmas Day, but it wasn't, I was just happy and my spirits were high.

'Good morning mama, good morning papa,' I said giving them each a kiss.

Mama was trying to feed a soft boiled egg to baby Elizabeth whilst she sat wriggling in her highchair, and papa was reading his paper.

A week later, 1976 England.

'Good morning Miss Sofia,' said Lynsey. 'Would you like a boiled egg?'

'Yes please. May I have two?' I looked over at mama.

Taking a sip of her *gly'kaniso* flavoured tea she nodded a yes at Lynsey. Perhaps it was a Greek thing, but most of the Greek adults I knew loved the acquired taste and smell of aniseed flavoured tea. I adopted a love for it too, mama had introduced it to us as soon as we were born - favouring it over gripe-water to sooth an upset tummy.

Lynsey placed two eggs into my favourite eggcups and handed them over to me with a mug of warmed milk, something she had done for as long as I could remember. Lynsey was not only our cook, but a constant stability in our lives, she was someone we needed for our well being and strength. Always sure of finding her in the kitchen, my sisters and I would gather there to get away from our parents' disputes, or were drawn by the inviting smells that guaranteed solace and warmth; Lynsey welcomed us with *'comfort eating'*, as she called it, dishing out the treat of the day. Silent and loyal, she too understood the tension between mama and papa.

I turned my head first towards Irini then Christina giving them that look that meant we knew something was wrong between our parents.

'Why is mama not speaking?' I whispered, looking down at my napkin. Irini shrugged her shoulders looking over at papa, and guessing from the tired look on mama's face, she hadn't had much sleep last night. Christina anxiously glanced from beneath her fringe as she uncomfortably bit into her toast.

'Mrs Bradshaw, would you please take Elizabeth to the playroom? I think she's had enough.' Mama said, drinking a little more tea.

Taking himself away from his newspaper for a moment papa looked up at her 'Go back to bed Elena. You look tired and pale my sweetness.'

'Yes I will, once I've said goodbye to the girls Harry.' She took one last sip. 'Will you be taking them to school today?'

'Yes. I've asked Mr Bradshaw to help me clear the remains of last night's bonfire at your mama's,' he said, reminding us of the glorious day we had had.

When he finished reading about the rise and fall of interest rates, we were ready to go.

'Now, get yourself to bed,' he said again and folding his newspaper

16

A week later, 1976 England.

he stood up, brushed himself down, walked over and kissed her on the forehead.

She never hesitated to take him up on his advice, and as soon as we were in the car and out of sight she'd headed for her room. Gone were the days when she needed to work - papa had made sure of that. After twelve years of investing in shrewd business deals he had become landlord to over fifty properties. But it wasn't always that way, the stories he told us of his childhood where so sad I sometimes couldn't sleep at night and would have had to climb into bed with mama to lay in her arms where I felt warm and safe, wondering what life must have been like for him not to be able to do that with his *mitera*.

The image of my papa, that scrawny little boy with his small case, an orange and some bread getting on the bus haunted me for years. Such a sad and abandoned child being driven so far away from home, so far from his *mitera*. I tried to sometimes feel what my papa must have been feeling and I'd be left with such a sorrow and emptiness in my stomach which used to reduce me to tears.

Christmas, December 1976 England.

Chapter Three

November had been a slow never-ending month, and with Christmas only a week away, it was our last day at school before the holidays. This day always began traditionally with Christmas hymns followed by a Nativity play. Each year proud parents gathered into the hall as Mrs Hodges, our music teacher, played tunes on her piano.

Mrs Hodges was a strange looking woman, quite scary with thin bony fingers, huge bulging eyes and yellowy-grey tinted hair. I didn't really like her much, she frightened me!

I liked our headmistress, Mrs Fairchild, she wasn't at all scary. She used to swan around school with a fixed smile on her face as if she didn't have a care in the world, always happy and cheery. Not even the bitter wind could dampen her mood; she stood near the open doors of the assembly hall and welcomed each parent equally. The only time Mrs Fairchild's smile disappeared was when she suspected foul play, which resulted in 'the suspect' being sent to her room to be punished. I very rarely got sent to her room, but there was one incident I try hard to forget when Christina had been asked by Miss Carter if she would kindly take Susanne Harris's art work to her home because she'd forgotten it and it needed to be finished. Susanne Harris was my form teacher's daughter and being that she lived near the school Miss Carter had said, '*Mr Bradshaw would be passing by there anyway,*' but instead Christina panicked, and not wanting to ask Mr Bradshaw for this favour, she threw it into the playground hoping Miss Carter would not remember who she'd given it to.

The next day, when Susanne's work had been found by the caretaker, papa was called to the school. '*Both Christina and Sofia will have to be punished!*' He'd promised our headmistress, saying that we must have both been at fault because we did everything together. Never before had we seen him so angry, so enraged, so much so that we got sent to bed without supper.

Christmas, December 1976 England.

'It's okay,' mama had said, trying to reassure us as we fought back the tears, 'it will all be forgotten in the morning.'

But I wasn't crying because of what Christina had done, or that we'd made papa so angry, I was crying because I was scared I wouldn't be his special princess anymore - and that he wouldn't love me.

As I prepared to enter the stage, I tried erasing that day from my mind. Today was a special day; I'd been chosen to play the Spirit of *Christmas Present*, in Charles Dickens's immortal *A Christmas Carol*.

Mama had arrived with Aunt Demi and *yia'ya* and nothing was going to spoil it. I was so thrilled to have been chosen for this part, as I'd read the book three times, and it was a favourite of mine. May was to play Ebonize Scrooge; she looked so funny in her long white nightgown and hat. Mrs Fairchild had selected her out of a group of five hopeful boys because she showed natural talent and could play roles of any kind. So with the blinds pulled down to keep out the daylight, the hall came alive with a thousand Christmas lights that haunted the stage like spirits. Scrooge was to be visited by a ghost, his old friend and partner, Jacob Marley. 'You will be visited by three spirits,' Marley began.

By the end of the play the parents were left so flabbergasted they could hardly contain themselves, whistling and cheering; showing their appreciation with a standing ovation.

'Bravo!' Called out one father.

'Well done!' Shouted another, as we gave our final bow.

'More! More! More!' They all chanted.

I could see my mama and Aunt Demi standing, clapping and waving their hands with *yia'ya* by their side.

'God bless us! God bless everyone! MERRY CHRISTMAS!' We all shouted at the top of our voices!

The rest of the week went by fairly quickly; there was so much to do. Mama, Mrs Bradshaw and Lynsey filled the whole house with Christmas decorations. Whilst Mama always encouraged us to help with decorating the Christmas tree she never allowed us to climb the ladder after falling off it herself one year and spending Christmas with a sprained ankle and on crutches. Every year papa picked out the biggest

Christmas, December 1976 England.

Christmas tree from Guilbey Farm, and this year was no exception. We watched in wonder as he carried it home with help from the three burly farmers that worked there, taking it into the conservatory very carefully they stood it in the corner... it was enormous!

Mr Bradshaw was not around to lend a hand this morning because he'd left the house early to avoid the shoppers who would be flocking into town for their last minute bargains. Of course they needed nothing, their turkeys had been stuffed, presents had been wrapped and were tucked under over-decorated Christmas trees, but still they would be there for sure. He'd gone to fetch *yia'ya* Athena, she always came to stay over for the holidays, and the first thing she would do, before she'd even taken off her coat, would be to go straight to the kitchen and look in the refrigerator making sure mama had picked up the chicken she would be needing to make us the best *av'go lemono* soup in the world! It was a tradition mama had adopted from *yia'ya* Athena and we always ate it on Christmas morning before going to church.

We couldn't wait, for we knew that upon entering the dining room, our taste buds would be bursting with pleasure from the lemony citrus in the air, knowing too well that the fluffy rice sitting at the bottom of this creamy, egg delight was a culinary excellence of nothing other than complete satisfaction. But before *yia'ya* had even stepped through the front door, Christina, Irini and I had already begun arguing over who was to sleep with her in her bedroom on Christmas Eve. We bickered so much that mama had no choice but to ask Mrs Bradshaw to set up sleeping arrangements for all three of us on the floor.

I always got to lay in the middle, cuddling up to them both as we listened to her telling us stories about mystical, magical lands where only special children were allowed to visit and that's how Christmas always began, *yia'ya* telling us stories as we fell asleep waiting for the day to arrive.

'Would you and Miss Athena like some tea and Christmas cake?' Asked Lynsey as Athena entered the conservatory.

She'd finished her story telling for yet another Christmas Eve.

'Oh yes please Lynsey. You are a darling. Mama would you like some tea?' Asked Elena.

Christmas, December 1976 England.

'Why not? All this wrapping presents and telling stories is thirsty work,' she whispered, looking at her daughter from beneath her smile she asked, 'Elena.... is there something wrong my love, something you'd like to talk about?'

Elena was unaware of the melancholy she was carrying.

'No everything's fine mama. I'm just tired that's all,' Elena lied - she didn't want to say, not now, not before Christmas Day.

'We'll have our tea and then it's off to bed then,' said Athena, addressing Elena just like another caring mother would to her little girl. She would have to get to the bottom of her feelings another day. 'We have a busy day tomorrow.'

I heard *yia'ya* creep back into the room and get into bed, gradually falling asleep as the house fell into an eerie silence; so eerie, that one could almost imagine that Scrooge himself was roaming the hallways waiting for Christmas to arrive. But as the whole world slept, waiting, I could do nothing other than stir in my bed 'til the night eventually turned into day and everywhere was glowing from the warm sun that shone throughout the house.

I ran straight to the window and for a moment I couldn't move, scream or do anything; all I could do was stare - just stare! Christmas Day had arrived and brought with it SNOW! It was everywhere! I'd prayed for snow and there it was as if it knew.

I really wanted to scream out but instead I whispered, 'Christina, Irini, shall we wake *yia'ya?*'

'She's not in her bed, come on let's get up its Christmas Day!' Called Irini, throwing back the covers as she headed for the door.

'Wait for us Irini! Christina let's go!' I cried.

We followed her into the hall dodging past the little round tables that stood by every window, each one with a different shaped vase full to the brim with dried thistle, holly and mistletoe. They drove mama mad, for every time she walked past one of them, she would stop finding something wrong with the arrangement and spending hours rearranging them.

'Mama, papa!' We were calling at the top of our voices. 'Mama, its Christmas, it's Christmas Day!'

'Good morning my little princesses!' Papa laughed, as they came out of their bedroom, scooping all three of us into his arms.

21

Christmas, December 1976 England.

'Merry Christmas my sweet girls,' mama beamed, joining us with baby Elizabeth. 'Merry Christmas *yia'ya*,' I said, letting go of papa to put my arms around her. A wonderful scent of winter roses surrounded me.

'Merry Christmas Sofia. Elena, Harry, girls, let's go down to the conservatory and open our presents.'

Christina, Irini and I took hold of each other's hands as we began skipping together, singing: '*We wish you a Merry Christmas, we wish you a Merry Christmas*,' and as our skipping now turned into running, our song's velocity quickened. '*Good tidings we bring to you and your king. We wish you a Merry Christmas and a happy new year.*' We sang, laughing at the top of our voices, then we ran down the wide stairs towards the conservatory, we could still hear Elizabeth trying to join in, copying us and waving her tiny plump hands in the air. 'Merry Christmas Miss Sofia; Miss Christina…Miss Irini,' said Mr Bradshaw, as we swung him around, almost knocking him over.

'Merry Christmas Mr Bradshaw! Merry Christmas Mrs Bradshaw!' We called back.

'And a Merry Christmas to you too,' smiled Mrs Bradshaw.

Entering the conservatory, I stopped running and just stared up at the Christmas tree, my heart was thumping so fast I thought it was going to erupt. I'm sure no other day was as special as this one, maybe that's why it came at the end of the year, letting us wait, adding to the anticipation.

I dreamt of getting married here at Christmas one day, with snow, a big tree in the conservatory and everything decorated in white. Christina would be playing the piano and we'd all have *yia'ya's av'go lemono* soup. It would be the most perfect of perfect days.

Soon the family would be arriving and mama had asked them not to be late, because it was a well-known fact that Greeks were always late, '*Mr and Mrs Bradshaw will be serving Christmas lunch at two thirty*,' she'd told them.

I looked up at the grandfather clock in the hall, it was one o'clock so I ran up to my bedroom. We had just returned home from church and there was plenty of time, all I had to do was change into the dress *yia'ya* Athena had bought for me to wear. So instead of getting dressed straight away, I just sat, relaxing in my room for a while after all the morning's excitement, it was good to be alone.

Christmas, December 1976 England.

Mama sometimes found me sitting here; it was my favourite place, on my sofa by the window overlooking the back garden. I would lay here at night with the crochet blanket my Auntie Freda had made for me. Auntie Freda - papa's sister who lived in Cyprus - had given it to me the first time we'd visited her whilst on holiday there in 1973. *'I have made especially for you,'* she'd told me. *'Take back to England and when you are cold, wrap around you and I will be always keeping you warm like Cyprus sun.'*

That's exactly what I did whenever I felt tired or cold; I would wrap my blanket around me and feel the warm Cyprus sun.

So, wrapped and warm I lay, looking out at the garden where I spotted a solitary robin hopping over the ground. His red face and breast were so bright and he was so bold without a care in the world. I could only marvel at him as he amused himself by flying from one tree to another before finally landing on the stone bird bath and mistaking his reflection for another, he began his attack! I laughed as I watched him play.

'Sofia, are you in here?' Asked my cousin Helen, poking her head around the door. She entered my room with both arms cradling what looked like my Christmas present. I threw back my blanket and ran straight to her.

'Helen, what is it?! What is it?!' I screeched, examining the brightly coloured box.

'You'll have to open it to find out. But first...' she said, turning her cheek my way. 'First I want my Christmas kiss,' and it was only after we'd exchanged kisses did she let me have it.

'Now you can open your present,' she smiled, stretching out her arms. I took it and we sat down on my bed, peeling away layer after layer, 'til there was no more covering; my 'one hundredth' china doll. She was beautiful! I carefully opened the box, and very gently took her out trying not to spoil her golden ringlets and gorgeous red taffeta ball-gown.

'I love her! I love her!' I cried. 'She's wonderful! I'm going to call her Megan,' I said, holding her up in the air, spinning her in circles as I went from one end of my room to the other.

Then, all of a sudden I stopped in my tracks! My cousin Helen was here which meant the whole family were here too, and I still wasn't dressed. I threw Megan on my bed as I headed for the wardrobe.

'Helen, help me with my dress, hurry!' I said, taking it off the hanger and quickly stepping into it. 'Do it up. Quick please!'

She slowly pulled up the zipper, trying not to catch it; I turned around and caught a glimpse of my reflection in the mirror. Green and navy tartan with a creamy coloured petticoat stared back at me.

'You look beautiful!' She said, admiringly.

I stood there for a moment, appreciating her flattery. 'Do you like it?' I smiled. She grabbed hold of my hand as she pulled me away. 'Yes. Now let's go down!' She said.

'No wait!' I called. 'I want to take Megan.'

When we got downstairs we found the rest of the family standing in small groups in different parts of the house. Some were listening, while others were doing all the talking. I greeted each of them individually with a kiss, we then headed for the conservatory where we found Christina sitting on her knees on the floor with little Anna, playing snakes and ladders. Fivo was playing a football board game with Kiri, although it wouldn't have been impossible to play the real thing in such a huge room as this. And as for Irini, she had dragged herself away from one of her novels and was laying on a rug by the Christmas tree trying to beat Christos at chess.

'Look at the china doll Auntie Maritsa and Uncle George have bought for me.' I said, holding up Megan, pointing her first in Christina's direction then Irini's.

'Sofia, mama said we weren't to open our presents from the family 'til after dinner. You're going to be in big trouble now,' Irini said looking up, taking great pleasure in reminding me of mama's rules.

'No I won't be.'

'Yes you will.'

'Mama didn't say that. Did she?' I asked, looking over at Christina.

'I didn't say what Sofia?' Mama said, startling me as she entered the conservatory so quietly.

'She's opened her present from Auntie Maritsa and Uncle George,' Irini informed her before I could even open my mouth.

'Irini, I didn't ask you. Now can you all make your way to the dining room please while I speak to Sofia,' she said.

When the conservatory had emptied and there was only the two of us, she went straight to the sofa and sat down.

'Come here Sofia,' she said calmly, giving the sofa a gentle pat.

I walked over and sat with her.

'She's very beautiful,' she smiled, stroking my doll.

I gave a knowing nod.

'It's okay Sofia, you're not in trouble,' she said, taking hold of my hand. 'But you really should have waited,' she whispered, secretly glad to have a moment somewhere quiet.

'I know, and I'm sorry mama.'

'Let's keep this between you and me.'

I agreed but just as she said it, we both looked up to find papa standing in the room.

'Is there a problem Elena?' He asked, concerned as to why we hadn't joined the rest of the family in the dining room.

'No, everything's just fine Harry,' she said, squeezing my hand. 'Come on lets go, everyone's waiting.'

Dinner parties at our house weren't formal or stuffy; in fact they were quite fabulous, very different from dinner parties held by other members of the family. The long walnut and rosewood table in the dining room looked so luxurious, dressed with mama's finest Royal Dolton, sparkling crystal glasses, polished silver cutlery and the candelabras, that were now ablaze, were to die for! I loved helping Lynsey with the centre piece; the flower arrangement always looked so incredible, dominating the table with elegance.

Everybody sat at their set places waiting for mama and papa to welcome them with a toast, beginning the celebration of Christmas Day. So, with their glasses filled with the best champagne, they raised them to welcome the family.

Christmas Day lunch was always taken in turns and this year was ours, though it didn't really matter whose house we were at, the food would be the same, the conversation would be the same, the jokes would be the same, because wealthy or not, Greeks loved life, and they loved to eat, and if anyone other than a Greek had the opportunity to eat in the company of Greeks, they would tell you it was an experience not quickly forgotten. As well as the turkey, roast potatoes and all the trimmings, we would also be having hundreds of traditional Greek dishes. So, keeping to yet another family tradition, this would be no ordinary Christmas meal.

First, Mr and Mrs Bradshaw served some more of *yia'ya's av'go lemono* soup, then, they brought in trays and trays of small dishes filled with the most scrumptious *meze'thakia*, and two large platters, one with pheasant, the other with hare that papa had brought home after a days' game shooting at Guilbey Farm. I, of course, didn't approve of such sport and always tried to avoid being around when he returned home proudly holding what he called, '*a successful day*'. After we were served all the scrumptious dishes, papa carved the traditional gigantic turkey, and we began tucking into a feast that was fit for a thousand kings; all except for papa that was! 'Mr Bradshaw,' he said, seriously placing down his knife and fork.

With a single nod to papa he left the room only to return with a further little dish which he placed in front of him. Mama put down her knife and fork and stopped eating, wondering what papa was up to now, and as Mr Bradshaw slowly lifted the lid to a huge roar of laughter and cheers, one knew papa was up to one of his mischievous tricks again. 'Now for the snails,' announced papa, playfully looking at the boys. 'I'll give five pounds to the bravest boy here. Who will it be?' He laughed out loudly, picking one up and pulling it out of its shell with a cocktail stick. 'Five pounds,' he said again, looking at Christos. 'Or will it be you,' he pointed it at Kiri, then at Fivo. Kiri burst into tears, he was, the youngest of the three.

'I don't like snails!' He cried, his frowning little face spoke for itself.

'If you eat this you will become a man,' jested papa.

'I'm only eleven; I don't want to be a man.'

'What about you Christos?'

Christos didn't reply he buried a worried looking face into Auntie Stella's huge bosoms.

'It will have to be Fivo then!' He said, handing it over to Uncle Nick.

Uncle Nick twiddled his moustache, took it from papa then dangled it in front of poor Fivo's face. I thought I was going to be sick, just the idea of having a snail in my mouth made my stomach turn, but everybody else was finding it all quite entertaining. Fivo took it from Uncle Nick, and with a glass of water in one hand and the snail in the other, he squeezed shut his eyes really tightly and the creature

Christmas, December 1976 England.

was gone! He raised his arms up in triumph, punching the air with his fists, and then he put one hand out to papa and laughed.

'Five pounds please Uncle Harry!'

Papa took five pounds out of his pocket, and as promised, gave it to Fivo, then with a huge satisfied smile, he gave the same to the rest of us. By the time everyone had finished eating, drinking and laughing, we'd almost forgotten it was baby Elizabeth's birthday.

'Would you like Lynsey to bring Elizabeth's cake in now?' Mrs Bradshaw reminded mama.

'Harry shall we go into the sitting room?' Asked mama, interrupting him from the deep conversation he was having with Uncle Mike.

'Yes Elena, if everyone has finished eating my love,' he said, breaking his conversation.

'Mama, can we open our presents first?' Christina asked with a desperate smile on her face. 'Please, can we?'

'Soon Christina, soon,' she reassured her. 'We'll have our tea and coffees in the sitting room please Mrs Bradshaw.'

'Yes, Miss Elena, right away.'

It was so difficult not to be fond of this room, with its fine antiques, china cabinets and great log fireplace. It always embraced us with an orange and cinnamon smell that was constantly released from the oil soaked dried flowers everywhere. I loved to sit on the thick carpeted floor close to the fireplace so I could listen to the logs crackling in the flames; it always reminded me of when I was really little, probably around six or seven and mama allowed me to sit in here while Christina was having her piano lessons. I think that's when my love for china dolls first began. My papa had bought a cabinet for mama one year for her birthday because she'd once told him about her rich Aunt Maro who had one that was filled with dolls from all around the world, saying *'I'd like one like hers'*. I would sit here for hours on the floor listening to Christina play the same tunes, over and over whilst admiring the china dolls - nothing had changed.

So, with the lights dimmed, and Christina sitting at the piano, we waited for Lynsey to make her grand entrance with Elizabeth's cake.

'Happy Birthday to you,' Lynsey began to sing as she entered the

27

Christmas, December 1976 England.

room. The log fire and the small flickering candles on the cake that shone in Lynsey's face were the only two things giving light to this enchanted room. She put the cake down carefully on a small round, *Lefka'ridiko* lace covered table in the middle of the room as Christina started to play and we all joined her singing, '*Happy birthday to you...*'

We were singing and clapping our hands as Elizabeth stared hypnotically down at the candles, and when we'd finished she blew them out, and with one tiny scoop, her little fingers were in the cake and then straight into her mouth. The laughter that circled around the room made her think she'd done something so clever and not to disappoint us she did it again....she was so funny!

It was Elizabeth's second birthday and mama had dressed her in the most gorgeous little baby blue dress she'd bought on a shopping trip to Paris with Aunt Demi. She looked so cute, fat and rosy cheeked with long blonde hair. She and I looked so alike; we were the image of mama with our fair porcelain skin and blue eyes. Irini resembled papa's side of the family, rather beautiful with her dark hair and Mediterranean looks Christina was a mixture of both, inheriting mama's fair complexion and papa's dark hair that complimented her features and big green eyes. I looked around me as my family sang together on this marvellous Christmas gathering and thought how privileged I was, it seemed we had it all.

Nothing could spoil this night, nothing could be more complete and as the night closed in all around us we could hear the sound of the howling wind tapping at the windows that had been drowned out by our singing. It was so cold outside that not even the suns strong rays, which had shone throughout the house all day, had softened the crystal icicles hanging from the trees. Too soon, the huge golden sun began waving us goodbye as it began its descent over the horizon, giving way for the moon, leaving behind a breath-taking sky that was filled with clouds of amber and crimson.

I faintly heard the grandfather clock in the hall ringing, its bells saying it was nearly time for bed, but I must have already fallen asleep on the floor by the warm log fire because I awoke in papa's embrace as he was trying to wake me up, beckoning me to go to bed. I opened my eyes to find him looking lovingly down at me and I tightened my hold. I loved being in his strong embrace, he reminded me of an ancient Greek warrior

Christmas, December 1976 England.

from Troy with his dark wavy hair and tall athletic build - I felt so safe, like nothing and nobody could ever hurt me.

So there I was, fourteen years old and still being guided by his lead whilst mama followed close behind. He tenderly kissed me goodnight and left mama to tuck me in.

'Goodnight papa, I love you,' I mumbled.

Mama gently tugged at my dress and replaced it with my nightgown.

'I love you mama,' I sleepily whispered.

'I love you too, Sofia,' she said as she pulled my satin blanket over me kissing me on the forehead then left.

I gradually fell back to sleep listening to the comforting murmuring sounds that were coming from downstairs, only the men's voices could be heard as they sat in the games room around a table where they were enjoying a hard game of poker. I could envisage them smoking their large Cuban cigars and drinking Cypriot Brandy. One could have mistaken that room for a casino in Monte Carlo where papa and his friends had spent many an enjoyable weekend. Also as their debates got louder and louder one may have thought they were rowing. Yet, everything Greeks did was done with passion as they put the world to rights.

The women, on the other hand, sat happily gossiping in the sitting room, eating *baklava* and drinking Cypriot coffee. My Auntie Stella would no doubt be pretending to understand the meanings of the coffee powder that sat at the bottom of their cups, making up stories about huge fortunes they were about to receive, and long and wonderful journeys they were going to embark on, sometimes even suggesting the possibility of perhaps a thrilling romance, which always guaranteed a great deal of joviality.

It didn't seem like I had been asleep for a long time, but the sun was about to rise and Henry, the cockerel from Guilbey Farm, began making his early morning call. I listened as one by one, my family found their rooms, and the house slowly fell into a peaceful slumber.

The only sound now was that of rain as it poured through the opened heavens above, and the grandfather clock ticking its tune; its bells ringing so loud they woke me from the restless dreams. I was hardly able to move my legs and began to panic, 'Papa!' I called. But

29

Christmas, December 1976 England.

he didn't hear me. 'Papa!' I called out for him again. He always came to my side whenever I had a bad dream, rushing to my room making everything okay, but he didn't come this time! I sat up in near darkness, trying to calm myself down. The cold air hit me as I pushed back my covers and gasping a deep breath I got out of bed. The stillness around me was so calming that I almost forgot my fears of the dark. The softly lit lamp, which was kept on in my room throughout the night, helped guide through the darkness. I entered the long hall wanting only to call him again, wanting to call him because I needed him, and I was about to, but I noticed his bedroom door slightly ajar, so instead, I quietly tip-toed towards it, peeking through the tiny opening. I gently put my face up to the door, and realising he wasn't in his bed, I closed it carefully trying not to disturb mama. I was sure he would be in the summerhouse, a place where we went to when either of us couldn't sleep. Papa would even go and sit in there when it was raining, he loved the sound of the rain crushing down on its roof, and it gave him peace of mind when he'd had a stress filled day at work.

I was so eager to find him I started to run, and failed to see the foot of the *chais- longue* at the bottom of the stairs. Kicking it I lost my balance and as I heard the thunder roar - I tumbled to the floor.

'Papa, papa!' I began a pitiful cry and picking myself up I noticed my knee was cut and bleeding. I started to hop towards the kitchen in search of something to wash it with. If only I could have known that everything I believed in, everything good in my life had been a lie and that nothing was as it really seemed, for what I was about to witness was worse than any nightmare.

I entered the kitchen and froze at the image that was unfolding before me. All I could do was stare through the window as the rain struck down, stare towards the summerhouse, numb and bewildered, my legs becoming completely lifeless as I opened the garden door that would lead me to him, lead me to the unknown. Never had I been more afraid than this moment here, right now, and as I got nearer, the more frightened I became. I could hear them laughing as they sat uncomfortably close to one another - my papa and Aunt Demi, he was stroking her face, looking into her eyes, he leant forward to whisper something in her ear and then...he *kissed* her! I turned my back on

30

Christmas, December 1976 England.

them not knowing what to do, I scampered back inside not wanting to be part of his betrayal. My heart was beating so fast I could hardly breathe as it pounded at my chest forcing it's way out. I found myself back in the dark kitchen my thoughts running away with me, I was sick with guilt and shaking all over.

'*How could he? How dare he?*' I wanted to scream out.

Did mama know? What if she did? What if everybody knew? Burying my face into my hands, I started to cry.

'Sofia, is that you my dear child?'

I looked up and to my relief I saw my *yia'ya* Athena, I ran straight into her arms sobbing uncontrollably.

'What is it Sofia? What's wrong my child?' She asked, taking out a handkerchief from her pocket to wipe away my tears. 'Is this why you are crying?' She said, examining my knee.

'Yes *yia'ya*,' I lied, hesitantly.

'What on earth are you doing getting up so early? Let's go to the bathroom and clean it up. You must get back to bed.'

'Can I sleep with you *yia'ya?*' I asked.

'Of course you can my child,' she smiled, wrapping a protective arm around my shoulder as we began our silent walk, leaving behind their deceit. *Yia'ya* reassured me all would be okay as I held on to her tightly, but I knew differently.

I turned my head to look behind; I knew then nothing would ever be the same again.

The final week of our Christmas holiday became a total blur. Hardly noticing anyone or anything, I spent most of the time in my room only coming out when mama called me down for supper. My silent behaviour was becoming a problem; it was making mama and papa sick with worry, but I wanted to be left alone with my thoughts and my nightmare; it was the only way I knew how to cope with it all.

For days, my mind went around in circles trying to make sense of it all, trying to put dates to events and as bit by bit it started to unfold, I remembered all the sudden business meetings with unnamed clients and the unacceptable reasons for being home late. I felt as though I'd lost my best friend - my rock. Who was this '*papa*' playing happy families with us? I wasn't too sure that I knew anymore, he had become a stranger.

31

Christmas, December 1976 England.

When and where did this affair first begin? When did my mama stop being his 'princess'? I desperately needed to know. Then, out of the blue, it hit like a bolt of lightening. As I lay on my sofa gathering my heartrending thoughts, a voice in my head said: '*25th December, 1974; the day my sister Elizabeth was born.*' I remember mama hadn't stopped running around all week. She was so busy trying to organize the event of the year in the Constantine household that she'd almost forgotten she was nearly nine months pregnant and making herself so ill our family doctor had no choice but to send her to bed.

'But I can't go to bed Dr Edwards,' she tried to explain. 'It's Harry's fortieth birthday next week, there's still so much to do,' she went on, trying to convince him otherwise.

'Yes maybe Elena, but that will have to wait!' Was what he'd answered. His strict reply wasn't what she wanted to hear, but to Mama's frustration, she did as she was told.

Later that day, and two weeks too soon, my baby sister Elizabeth was born and just as Dr Edwards had said; '*Papa's birthday will indeed have to wait.*'

'Mama had asked papa to inform the rest of the family telling them of the good news. 'Telephone my mama, tell her Mr Bradshaw will be collecting her,' she said, holding her huge belly as he helped her into the car. 'And don't forget Maritsa and Stella, Oh, and my cousin....'

'Elena stop worrying, I will call everyone,' he interrupted, reassuring her he had everything under control. 'Now get in the car my love.' She turned and looked at him, giving him a look of '*please don't forget*'.

'Yes, I won't forget your cousin Mike,' he said, calming her as he helped her into the seat. Christina, Irini and I stood with Lynsey and Mrs Bradshaw watching as Mr Bradshaw drove them away.

Later that same day after telephoning Elena's sisters, Harry continued to do as he'd promised and he telephoned Mike...

'Hello Mike, its Harry. Elena's in hospital she's had the baby.' He exclaimed.

'That's fantastic news cousin! What did she have?'

'A girl, she had a beautiful baby girl, Elizabeth!'

'Well, you can't be by yourselves tonight, it's Christmas Day. Come over to us.'

'No cousin I think it'll be better for you to come here, the girls are with me and Athena is coming over and Lynsey's also cooked a wonderful supper.'

'Okay, but you must let Demi and I take you out for a celebratory drink first. We'll pick you up at eight o'clock.'

It must have been past midnight when they returned home because *yia'ya* had said we could stay up and wait for papa but by eleven thirty we were so tired she sent us to bed. I remember hearing papa helping Uncle Mike to his room after he'd obviously had too much to drink. I'd woken up thirsty and called out to him. After helping Uncle Mike to bed he then fetched me some water saying he had to return downstairs to Aunt Demi. I thought nothing of it at the time. Why would I have? Papa was helping Uncle Mike to bed and he was going back to our Aunt Demi - as any good host would. I wasn't aware what had happened that night would change the future forever.

Demi sat in the sitting room waiting for Harry to return. After two bottles of Champagne, which was devoured between the three of them, she was feeling a bit light headed.

'He'll be fine in the morning,' he said, re-entering the room heading straight to the log fire. 'Are you cold, Demi?' He poked the logs, without a glance to her.

'No, I'm fine,' she replied, taking a slow sip of her Champagne. It felt cold on her lips, then cool in her mouth, but with the endless flow and the heat from the log fire she was beginning to feel uncomfortable so removed her jacket. Harry stood up, walked over to where he'd left his drink and poured himself another.

'Would you like a fresh one?' He asked, pouring carefully as his hand began to tremble.

'Need some help?' She teased.

He stopped pouring, looked at her and smiled. 'No I think I can manage,' he said, holding up the bottle and giving it a shake. 'One more?'

'Yes, I will have another. Why not?'

He filled two glasses. 'Thanks,' she said, her green eyes reflecting in his as she stared straight up at him. Then reaching up to take the glass, she cradled both hands over it, playfully stroking his fingers. He stood over her, fully aware of her thoughts, but with so much anxiety

Christmas, December 1976 England.

in the room they were both too afraid to speak, for they knew what might happen if they dare.

'What's bothering you Demi?' He said, feeling her tension.

'Nothing. I've had a headache all week,' she replied, taking her hands off of his.

'Why? Who's been on your mind?' He asked, turning away from her to sit on the opposite sofa.

'Don't you mean what?' She inquired as her stare fell to the ground.

'No I don't. I mean who?'

She didn't answer straight away; her pause focused to the ground and then she just said it.

'You,' she replied, 'I've been thinking of you, Harry. You've been on my mind.'

'What have you been thinking?' He asked. He wanted to hear her say what he already knew.

Biting her bottom lip, unable to look at him, she said; 'I've been thinking about you and me; Elena and Mike. I can't help but think that if the two of us had met first,' she replied turning her head to look at him now.

'And what if we had? Would things have been different?

'Don't make this anymore difficult for me, Harry, than it already is,' she said.

'You mean better,' he corrected her, 'not difficult.'

'No. I'm not sure. I just wonder sometimes. Don't you?'

'What? Different or better?' He said, finishing his glass and getting up to pour himself another.

'Stop playing with me Harry,' she said, looking at him, suddenly becoming scared of what she had started. It was all getting a bit too much for her now. Standing, still holding her glass she walked over to the fireplace and just stared at herself in the mirror. He walked towards her.

'Who's playing?' He said, taking the glass from her hand, placing it on the mantelpiece. He then raised her head up so he could kiss her, but she turned the other way. 'Now who's playing?' He asked and lifted her into his arms, carrying her into summerhouse to where they were to make love for the very first time.

34

Spring, March 1977, England.

Chapter Four

I felt the warm air that had arrived with spring travelling over my face, as I sat under the weeping willow tree, that overlooked the pond in a secluded part of our garden. It brought with it the aroma of freshly cut grass, and I could imagine the sound of the lawn mower as it shaved the spiky green fibres with its sharp blades, reminding me of sports day and slices of juicy ripe water melon. I was at peace with the world here, as this is where I would escape with my canvas and oils.

Hoping Christina and Irini wouldn't disturb me, I began to paint another one of my great masterpieces, the only sound to be heard was that of ducks as they bobbed and dived from the surface of the pond, searching for water plants and small animals to feed on. I stopped to watch them as they splashed their webbed feet, going under for a swim and then leaping in the air, becoming airborne.

Putting down my paint brush for a minute, I sat staring into the distance, not actually looking at any one single thing, just staring into nothingness as the pond and the ducks merged into one. Feeling a little dizzy, I laid down on the grass holding my head; papa and Aunt Demi entered my mind.

It was still difficult at times to forget what I'd seen on that dreadful night last Christmas. The images of them together in the summerhouse were still so vivid and disturbing that I sometimes wanted to scream out aloud, hoping it might make them go away. I wasn't sure how long I could keep it to myself. I needed to tell someone for fear I'd go mad. But, pretending it had never happened, and that papa still belonged to us, was made easier on days like these when I could put the winter nights behind me; making it all seem a million miles away.

'Get up lazy; we've got work to do. Miss Carter will send us to Mrs Fairchild if it's not in on Monday,' said May, standing over me holding her canvas in one hand and a wicker basket in the other.

'Yes and today's Saturday. We've plenty of time,' I replied.

Spring, March 1977, England.

She placed her canvas next to mine, then sat down beside me, took out a yellow gingham table cloth from her basket and laid it neatly on the ground.

'Are you hungry?' She asked. 'There's hard boiled eggs, black olives, home-made bread with tomatoes and fresh iced lemonade.'

Not wanting to move, I replied, 'No. Just lay here with me May.'

Quite happy with just relaxing under the long greenish-yellow shoots that hung straight down from the dome shaped willow tree that was shading us from the dazzling sky, we took a moment just lying next to one another without uttering a word.

'Jonathan asked after you,' May said breaking the tranquil silence.

'Jonathan who?' I asked, knowing exactly what her reply would be.

'Jonathan Guilbey, silly,' she answered, giving me a familiar nudge.

'What did he say?'

'He asked how you were. Anyway, I thought you didn't like him, I thought you didn't care?'

'I don't... well I do... he is okay I suppose. You know my papa doesn't allow us to speak with boys, and especially non-Greeks.'

'What about George Parras? What will he think when he finds out you like Jonathan?'

'He won't find out because there's nothing to find out. I just think he's okay.'

'Your papa thinks George would be a good match for you.'

'Well I'm not ready for papa's match making. Though I do think George is cute. He's very handsome. Don't you think?'

'What do I think, Jonathan? George? George? Jonathan? Who will it be?' she laughed, finding the whole thing quite amusing.

'Go on laugh, but it's not funny. Wait 'til it happens to you,' I laughed, giving her back one of her nudges.

'I won't let my papa dictate to me who I will fall in love with and marry, that would be hypocritical being that he married my mum who, I'm sure, was brought up with different values and traditions to him.'

Perhaps she was right, I thought, maybe May wouldn't have to abide by Greek rules being that her papa, Sotiri Iouanou, had fallen in love with an English lady called Diane - after meeting her at their local dance hall in the early sixties - whom he had dated for six months before introducing her to his family, announcing to them that Diane was pregnant and that they were to be married before the baby was born. He was one of many Greek men that, upon setting foot in England, had met and married a non-Greek girl.

Scared of saying any more, I closed my eyes and let out a deep sigh of frustration because I wanted to tell her, I needed to if I was to be rid of this nightmare finally. I imagined what her reaction would be; the look of horror on her face when she found out; the disgust and the disappointment: *'Tell her now,'* I said to myself: *'Just say it.'*

I turned and looked at her, hoping our special telepathy would help me; I waited for a sign that said she was aware of my thoughts; but there was nothing.

'May, I've got something to tell you,' I began, when all of a sudden I heard our names being called.

'Sofia! May!' They were shouting out loudly. I stopped and sat up. I could see Christina and Irini.

'Sofia! May! Sofia! May!' They screamed, their voices getting louder and louder.

They were coming so fast down hill that they eventually came to a halt, out of breath and exhausted, both falling at our feet as they burst into hysterical fits of laughter.

'Well....have you finished your masterpieces?' Irini asked sarcastically, looking over at our canvases. 'I thought not,' she said. 'What have you both been doing all this time?'

'Probably talking about boys,' sniggered Christina. Yet even through sarcastic sniggers neither had a mean bone in their bodies.

'Bet you were talking about George Parras. Hey Sofia?' Irini smirked.

May opened her eyes, and without moving an inch, looked over at them both and asked. 'What about you Christina. Do you still want to marry his brother?'

'Yes I do. I'm going to marry Anthony and Sofia's going to marry George,' she replied, swaying her head from side to side, sticking her nose in the air.

'Oh *really*? Is that right?' She said, looking down at me as I lay facing her on the ground. Our eyes met and I gave May that look. She knew not to mention Jonathan because I hadn't told my sisters I liked him just in case they let it accidentally slip and papa found out. 'What about you Irini,' May continued her interrogation. 'Have you found

37

Prince Charming yet?'

'No I haven't,' she replied, and refusing to go further with May's cross-examination, she got up and started to run. 'Come on! Let's go to Guilbey Farm!' She called out. 'Last one there's a sissy!'

We scrambled to our feet and ran, as we'd often done, like crazy to the bottom of the garden. One after the other we climbed over the tall fence falling into the uncut grass below, our hearts pulsating with the knowledge of our enthused adventure as we ran with heavy steps through the overgrown field beneath our feet.

With the wind in my hair, I raised my arms up, letting my feet take me on my flight. I was free, as free as a *Holly Blue*, in her innocence.

'Let's play 'hide and seek!' Yelled May.

'Yes, let's!' I called back and as we got closer to the farm we all headed in different directions.

The poor chickens and geese that we'd disturbed, had become so terrified of our presence they began running for their lives, clucking and flapping their wings, frantically dodging out of our paths. When I stopped running I hid behind the first little chicken shed I came across, and with my stomach full of exuberance, I struggled to calm myself down.

'Got you!' Said a voice I wasn't expecting to hear, and taking hold of my hand, he pulled me to the other side of the shed so that no one would see us.

'Jonathan!' I cried. I was half excited, half shocked.

'Shh.' He said, putting his hand up to my mouth, 'I wanted to catch you by yourself.'

'Why Jonathan?' I asked, keeping away from his gaze because I couldn't look into his eyes; his gorgeous, piercing blue eyes.

He leant forward, and without warning he gave me a kiss.

'Happy birthday for Monday,' he unexpectedly whispered. Then before I knew it he was gone. I searched all around for him but he was no-where to be seen, and even though I could still feel his kiss on my cheek, I put my hand up to my face, wondering if I had imagined him, if I had been daydreaming again. I smiled.

'Sofia! Sofia, what are you doing?!' Screamed Christina, grabbing hold of my arm.

'Come on, let's find the others.'

Spring, March 1977, England.

I just looked at her, with a fixed smile.

'Come on,' she said again, tugging me.

Slowly we moved through the farm like two foxes in search for our prey. Letting her guide me - for my mind was still somewhere else - she gave my hand another tug, then a squeeze, telling me she'd spotted someone by the old yew tree, and a pair of feet belonging to May were now in full view and with one swoop it was done!

'I'm the winner! I'm the winner!' Shrieked Irini jumping up and down, punching her fists in the air.

'Come on, we should be getting back,' I said.

It was getting late, and with all the madness of the day, we'd completely lost track of time and soon it would be dark. So feeling tired and hungry we made our way back leaving the chickens and geese in peace for at least another day. Even though the sun had gone down, and it was quite chilly now, I had a warm feeling inside of me. A feeling that said: I like Jonathan Guilbey, I like him a lot!

*   *   *   *   *   *   *   *   *

The next day, once again my papa was playing a different role, one of an adulterer and a liar. Demi sat patiently waiting for him in his apartment in the South East of London, one he'd bought especially for their meetings. It was a place where they would go on a regular basis for an hour or so stealing time here and there when they could. Overlooking the splendid river Thames with its historic excellence, it was of the highest quality and the best that money could buy. The spectacular skyline from across this winding waterway was a mixture of old and new, so full of history, traditions and customs. With the OXO building and St Paul's Cathedral blending into Houses of Parliament and the brilliant Savoy, it was truly breathtaking.

She'd made up a not so convincing story, but one that he trusted about why she was unable to attend church that morning, telling Mike a work colleague of hers had separated from her boyfriend and was so heartbroken she desperately needed to see a friendly face. Only the eccentric looking woman who lived in the next apartment had seen them come and go. She had introduced herself to Harry that

39

Spring, March 1977, England.

morning as he entered the lift.

'Good morning,' she smiled, looking at him inquisitively. 'I'm Mary and this is my baby, Missy,' she informed Harry, referring to the little dog she was carrying in her handbag. 'I named her that because she's such a spoilt little madam. Top floor?' She asked keeping her finger pressed on the button; there was no need to, she already knew. 'Yes please,' he replied, a little agitated.

She made him feel especially nervous, so he looked away hoping she would continue fussing over her 'baby', and that by some miracle she'd stop talking to him. But she didn't stop and in that quick minute as the lift took them up to the eighth floor she'd managed to tell him her whole life story - she was a psychiatrist working for a private clinic in central London, a divorcee, who had left her doctor husband of twenty years because he'd gone mad and started running naked around the village where they had lived. When they finally got to their floor, the doors opened and they parted and with his adrenalin now racing, he began thinking about Demi and the image of her ready and waiting for him.

Wearing only the small silky negligee he'd bought for her, Demi took a last glance at herself in the long mirror in the bedroom, and pleased with the reflection looking back at her, she hoped he would be too. She always made sure to do as he wanted, though it was sometimes hard to please such a worldly man; a man who could have any woman he pleased. She suspected she wasn't the only lover in his life. He had money, power, good looks and charm, what woman could resist him? He was used to always getting what he wanted, and he wanted her from the very first moment they'd laid eyes on each other.

'I thought you'd forgotten me,' she said, as he opened the front door

'*Demi*, how can a man forget such beauty?' He gave her a mischievous smile. Walking slowly towards her, he took his time, making her wait.

'Do you like what you see?' She asked, getting up and giving him a little twirl.

'Do I just. Come here.' He took hold of her hand and began by kissing every part of it, stroking her with his soft touch as his lips climbed higher and higher, finding her neck, then her mouth, he began to lead her into the bedroom, but to his surprise she pulled him to her.

40

Spring, March 1977, England.

'No Harry, kiss me here. Kiss me now,' she said. She wrapped her arms around him waiting and wanting only to please her, he seductively traced his fingers over her full, perfectly shaped lips, gently kissing her on the mouth, feeling the warmth of her breath on him. He pulled her closer and she began to tremble in his arms, he grabbed hold of her hair, the way she liked it, gently pulling her head back so he could look into her eyes, kissing her now with a passion like it was the first time. He then laid her down on the floor, and taking hold of her negligee he raised it up; her breaths were long and slow – he waited for her to ask him for more, looking deep in her eyes with a penetrating stare as he teasingly prepared her for a journey into ecstasy.

It was late by the time he'd finally decided to stroll home, but Elena was still up and waiting for him, sitting alone in her bed, reading a book. She'd never confronted him before and she wasn't about to start now, but Elena had lots of questions swimming around in her troubled mind, and pushing them back into her deepest fears only added more anxieties to her already depressive state. Confronting Harry meant accusing him, accusing him of things she wasn't prepared to find out. She loved him so much - he was her world, her first and only love. But he had changed, and a wife knows her own husband. This man that had come home tonight sitting beside her on their bed was not the same man she had married. Although he was still especially loving and caring, she knew there was a difference about him, a difference she could see in his eyes and feel in his touch. It had become a huge burden, carrying her fears around for the past year, and there were many times when she'd almost told Maritsa and Stella, though telling them would have made it all so final and irreversible that she couldn't bring herself to do it.

'Elena my love, why are you not sleeping?' He questioned, his mind refusing to believe she suspected foul play.

'I'm not tired. What time is it? Why are you late?' She said, throwing her arms around him as she began to sob.

'What's the matter my love? What's with the tears?'

'Do you love me Harry?' She asked, trying not to think about where he'd been.

'What kind of question is that?'

41

Spring, March 1977, England.

'Do you love me? That's all.'

He kissed her eyes and wiped away her tears.

'Like I've never loved another,' he replied. This was his wife, the mama of his children, how could he not love her? Cradling her tenderly in his arms he laid her down, feeling the comfort of their embrace with the only sound coming from their hearts beating together almost synchronized. Her body felt soft and warm as he slowly touched and caressed her, pulling her even closer as they began to kiss.

'I love you Harry,' she said in desperation.

'Don't say any more my love,' he kissed her.

Easter, April 1977, England.

Chapter Five

Miss Harris wrote the date on the blackboard, it read: MONDAY, 17th APRIL 1977. *'Monday, 17th April 1977,'* I repeated it to myself, writing it down in my exercise book. Today was my birthday; I was fifteen and had finally caught up with May, as she had beaten me to it six months ago. My only worry was break time; I was dreading going outside to the bumps. Having had to put up with enough traditions in my life, the bumps was one I could do without. The very thought of being thrown into the air fifteen times, with an extra one for luck, petrified me. I'd seen it all done before, and I didn't want to be a part of it, so I lied to Miss Harris, saying I wasn't feeling well; hoping she'd send me to Matron as my 'tummy ache' progressively became more severe. Matron had no choice but to phone mama to come and collect me from school early.

Sofia, Mr Bradshaw is coming to collect you,' Matron informed me on her return from the office, where she'd just been speaking to mama on the telephone.

'Thank you Matron,' I said, giving her a pitiful look.

'That's fine me dear, you just lay there. He'll be here soon,' she smiled, swivelling her chair around so she could get a better view as she looked out of the window.

Mrs Daniels, matron to us, was an Irish lady who was always full of beans, had an enormous heart and had been at our school forever. Originally from Southern Ireland, she constantly complained about, everything English really, telling us that one day, before she became very, very old, she would return to the land she called: *'a jewel.'*

'I think your Mr Bradshaw is here, me dear,' she said, still staring out of the window.

Holding my tummy, I pushed my feet into my shoes, took in a deep breath and began making my way down to meet him.

'Sofia!' Matron called for me to stop.

I turned around slowly and looked back at her. 'Yes, Matron?'

Easter, April 1977, England.

I asked.

'Happy birthday, me dear,' she smiled.

'Thanks, Matron,' and without another word I turned and left, though Matron and I knew why I was really going home.

I had to wait a whole week before I could celebrate my birthday with a party, and for that whole week I stayed at home hoping that by the time I returned to school my birthday would be forgotten along with the bumps. The only problem was, I hadn't seen Jonathan for six whole days and I needed to see him, so I was glad when the day had eventually arrived.

It wasn't unusual for the *whole* world to have received an invitation, but the only person I was glad to see was Jonathan. He arrived with his mother and father - typically British — early and looking quite the English gentlemen escorting his sister Sarah. I caught sight of them in the hall and I could see they seemed a little overwhelmed by the enormity of the whole event, so I quickly rushed over to rescue them.

'Happy birthday, lovey,' smiled Aunt Margaret.

'Thanks Aunt Margaret, you shouldn't have,' I said, accepting her kind gift with a kiss on both cheeks. 'Hello, Grandma Guilbey.'

'Happy birthday dear, you look lovely.'

'Thank you, grandma,' I replied, giving her a warm embrace.

'Fifteen, ay? Got a boyfriend yet?' Laughed Uncle Henry, planting one of his hearty kisses on my forehead.

Shaking my head with embarrassment, I mumbled, 'no Uncle Henry, not yet.'

I really liked Uncle Henry; he was a bit of a joker.

'Margaret, Henry, Grandma Guilbey, welcome. Come into the garden,' said mama, greeting them with open arms, subtly diverting them, sparing me further embarrassment from Uncle Henry.

'Happy birthday, Sofia,' smiled Sarah. However, just as Jonathan was about to speak to me, my cousins Helen and little Anna barged in between, pulling me away, leaving poor Jonathan and Sarah just standing like spare parts.

'Oh my God! *Who's that?*' Helen's voice shrieked with enthusiasm.

'You sly fox. You kept him quiet,' said little Anna, mimicking Helen's enthusiasm.

Easter, April 1977, England.

'That's Mr and Mrs Guilbey's son, Jonathan, from the farm next door,' I said, as they ushered me away.

'That's Jonathan? Well I expect an introduction later. You know, something like, 'this is my lovely cousin Helen."

'No, not your cousin Helen - your lovely cousin Anna,' she said, tugging at me. 'I don't remember him being that gorgeous.'

'Sorry, I think he already has a girlfriend,' I lied, hoping they wouldn't go on at me all day.

'That's just my luck, always too late,' said Helen.

'Never mind, George Parras will do. Quick! He's standing with his brother. Anthony, they're talking to Christina and Irini,' said little Anna, pulling us both with her.

Thankfully, I caught sight of May sitting by herself under the pergola that papa's grapevine from Cyprus had happily climbed over, creating the perfect place if you wanted to be in the shade. I freed myself from their tug of war, and went over to join her.

'Hey, where have you been?' She asked.

'Saying hello to the Guilbeys,' I said, kissing her.

'This looks great, doesn't it?' She observed, referring to the garden.

'Yes it does, my mama never does anything by half,' I agreed.

Mama loved throwing parties; birthdays, summer barbeques, Easter, Christmas, any excuse. I'm sure they got better as we got older or maybe it was just that we appreciated them more, and when the weather permitted, like today, she would make sure that everything was absolutely fabulous in this wonderful garden. With little round lace covered tables under trees, scattered blankets on the grass for us to sit on, and a million pink and white balloons tied to branches and trees, one could have very easily mistaken it for a painting by *Monet*; all that was missing were the vibrant orange-red poppies. The air was warm, filled with a pleasant fragrance of scented perfume that was now coming towards me from the sweet violets as they sat beside the nodding bluebells. I could see my favourite little yellow delights, the creeping buttercups and yellow, white and purple tips belonging to the tiny crocus' popped out from the grass. Huge daffodil lined boarders were everywhere, they even stood in rows beneath the stone bird bath where the jolly robin had made his mark last winter, having

45

now given way to the little sparrows sitting perched on the edge, dipping in their tiny beaks, wearing 'black bibs' as they quenched their thirst.

'D'you think we're going to eat today?' Laughed May, looking over at papa and Uncle Mike as they were frantically trying to keep the flames from the barbeque under control.

'No! Not if papa and Uncle Mike have anything to do it.'

'I see your cousins Helen and little Anna are driving poor George half crazy.'

'Erm, they're going to scare him if they don't stop.'

'No. He looks as though he loves the attention. But I do think all he really wants is to talk to you, poor guy,' she reminded me. 'Can you see him looking over at us?'

'There's Paris and Desy,' I said, waving at them taking no notice of her comments about George. 'They're here at last. Let's say hello.'

'Sofia! Happy birthday!' Yelled Paris. She had such an uncontrollable, infectious giggle, a giggle that had got us into trouble with Miss Harris many a time.

'Thanks, Paris.'

'A present from the both of us. Happy birthday!' Said Desy, giving me an odd looking parcel.

'Thanks you two, it looks fab!' I said.

I was really excited but still my mind was going round in circles as I wondered where Jonathan had got to. I needed to find him, so making up a poor excuse I headed for the house. On my way I passed Aunt Margaret, Uncle Henry, Sarah and Grandma Guilbey. They were sitting on some comfy chairs under the balloon covered oak tree talking with Auntie Stella and Uncle George. Grandma Guilbey was saying how a fox had come into the farm last night and taken her beloved cockerel Henry, leaving behind only the remains of a few feathers. She'd obviously been extremely traumatized by it all because she clearly looked upset and was trying to fight back the tears.

'Sorry about Henry, grandma,' I said.

'Oh, don't mind me, Sofia; you enjoy your party dear.'

'Have you seen Jonathan, Aunt Margaret?' I asked, trying not to sound too eager in front of Auntie Stella.

'No lovey, when your mother dragged us into the garden he

didn't come.'

'Yes,' replied Sarah. 'I left him indoors; I think he went into the conservatory.'

'I'll put this with the others,' I said, showing them the odd looking parcel.

And hoping no one else would stop to wish me a happy birthday, I hurried into the house as quickly as I could, running through the hall towards the conservatory, and as the clock rang its bells, striking the time, it startled me.

'Sofia! Up here!' Called a voice.

I looked up and there he was, standing on the landing, leaning over the banister, and with a quick sharp turn, I run up towards him.

'Jonathan! What are you doing up here?'

'I've been up here ages, waiting for you. What's that odd looking parcel you're holding?'

'I don't know! One of Paris and Desy's jokes no doubt. Come on, I'll put it with the others,' I said, grabbing hold of his arm as we started to run down the long corridor to my room.

'Wow!' He marvelled, as I opened my bedroom door.

Throwing the parcel on my bed as I headed for the window I said the first thing that came to my head. 'Look, you can see the farm from up here.'

'Sofia, see that small window to the left?'

'Yes,' I replied.

He was standing so close I could almost feel him breathing.

'That's my room.'

'Oh no!' I said, turning to face him.

'It's okay, I can't see you from there Sofia,' he laughed.

'You had me worried for a moment.'

'Who's she?' He asked, looking down at the doll sitting on my sofa wrapped in Auntie Freda's blanket.

'She's Megan, I got her last Christmas. Isn't she pretty?' I said, picking her up to show her to him.

'Yes she is. She looks like you.'

'Stop it,' I replied. I felt myself blush. 'You don't mean that, silly. She's beautiful. 'And so are you Sofia.'

I turned towards the window and continued looking outside down to where my family and friends were, I didn't know what to say and I didn't know what to do. *'Oh poor Uncle Mike,'* I thought, papa had left him alone with the barbeque, but he actually looked as though he was in control. At least now we weren't going to starve and May could stop worrying about her stomach.

I put Megan back down on the sofa next to Auntie Freda's blanket, and as I turned around I glanced up at the only poster I had on my wall and suddenly I blurted out, 'do you like David Cassidy?' cringing I muttered, 'why did I ask him that?'

'David who?' He shrugged, confused.

'David Cassidy. You know, The Partridge Family, *'I think I love you,'* I sang out of tune.

'Oh yes! I remember The Partridge Family. Don't tell anyone but I used to like his mother!' He laughed.

'That's terrible,' I teased.

'I know. You're the only one I've ever told.'

'Don't worry, your secret's safe with me...David Cassidy's mother?' I laughed with him. 'I've got their record here somewhere. Shall I play it?'

'No, it's okay. I'm well and truly over her now.'

'Really, are you sure?'

'I'm sure. There's only one girl for me,' he said.

'Oh, and who's that?' I asked, as I felt him take hold of my hand.

I wasn't sure what he was thinking or what he was about to say, but the uncomfortable atmosphere that had been present earlier had now disappeared, and as I looked into his gorgeous blue eyes, I knew I was falling for him. I'd always liked him but this felt different and I was hoping he'd kiss me again. I wanted him to; after all Saturday's kiss by the chicken shed didn't really count. *'Please kiss me,'* I thought.

'Princess?' Said my papa, as he swung open the door. 'What's going on Sofia?' He asked immediately. He had a terribly shocked look on his face - one of disgust.

'Nothing papa,' I answered, letting go of Jonathan's hand immediately.

He entered my room, walked calmly towards me and stood, waiting for an explanation.

'I'm sorry Mr Constantine, but Sofia was doing nothing wrong,' Jonathan said, trying to take control of what seemed to be turning into an unpleasant situation.

'I'm not speaking to you Jonathan,' he replied, still staring at me. 'Sofia, what's going on?' he asked again.

'Nothing papa.'

And with that he slapped my face, and I let out a scream putting my hand up to my cheek, and turning from Jonathan's gaze.

'Go downstairs Jonathan!' He ordered.

'But, Mr Constantine I can explain.'

'Downstairs!' He shouted.

'I can explain.'

'I said, *NOW*!'

Jonathan looked at me but he knew not to say anymore, he turned around slowly and left.

'What were you thinking Sofia?! What will the family think of your behaviour?! You have disgraced me!' He shouted some more. 'I will deal with Jonathan Guilbey later!'

I was so scared, I thought he might slap me again but instead he stormed off in a fury, slamming my door behind him, leaving me feeling ashamed - ashamed and embarrassed because I'd been bad. He had every right to be angry with me. I knew I wasn't to talk to boys, I understood that, but would Jonathan understand? I don't think he ever could. Papa had humiliated me in front of Jonathan and I don't even think he knew, nor cared.

I fell onto my sofa, wrapped myself with my blanket and started to cry. He'd never hit me before, but today I had been hit, today he'd shown me a different papa and I would have to accept the rules, I would have to accept, or there would be trouble. He'd shown me the rules today, as he too had been shown so many times, long ago.

Harry Constantine was just twelve years old when, for lack of money, he left school. His *mitera* got a visit from his teacher after receiving the bad news that he was leaving when the term was over. He pleaded with her to allow him to continue his studies.

'If he could stay until he's eighteen it would make such a difference,' he said. 'He's such a bright boy Mrs Constantine, it would be such a waste,' he told her.

She was just a simple, hard working woman with a poor, uneducated background who came from a small village, where if you had no

49

money, you left school as soon as possible and went off to work. If you were lucky, you went to the city where you would learn a trade. He'd made the long journey before with his *mitera*. She would go to Nicosia at least twice a year to buy the most sumptuous fabrics for her rich clients, from brocades and damasks, to rich golden silks. Being a seamstress to the wealthiest was not an easy task, they relied on her to bring them back only the very best. So, she packed his belongings in a small old case, gave him an orange and a slice of bread for the journey, one Greek shilling for the bus fare and waved him goodbye. As the bus pulled away, about to embark on a sweltering journey, Harry looked behind him, watching as Paphos disappeared into the distance, and he started to cry.

Mr Sava's wife, a lady from Nicosia's highest society, was there at the bus stop waiting for him to arrive.

'Hello, are you Harry?' she said, bending down to shake his hand. 'I'm Mrs Sava, but you can call me Theodora. Did you have a good journey?'

Harry looked down and just nodded, he could smell tobacco on her breath.

'You must be hungry, come, Maroulla's at home waiting,' she informed him taking his small case. 'Sit in the front with me.'

Opening the car door he could smell the same pungent stench of tobacco. Theodora had just lit a cigarette. He'd never seen a Greek woman smoke a cigarette before, his *mitera* didn't smoke, and neither did any of the women in the village where he lived, but this was not his village and this was not *his mitera*. And as he entered the roasting tin can, he sat watching with curiosity and sadness as Theodora drove him even further from his home. And all the way he could see residential houses and shops lining the streets; cafés packed with men of every age drinking coffee, playing backgammon and cards. The smell of succulent meat, going round on spits, entered the car. His tummy rumbled with hunger as he watched the cement covered workmen standing in small groups waiting for their lunch.

With the short bumpy ride over, the car came to a sudden halt, in front of a large white-washed stone house with green shutters and a black door. With the hand-break now secured, Theodora brushed her hair, and then took out a mint flavoured sweet from her handbag and popped it in her mouth to disguise the smell of tobacco on her breath. She gave one to

Easter, April 1977, England.

Harry as they got out of the car. Putting one hand on his bony shoulder, she held his little case with the other and began leading him through the multi-coloured garden. What a fantastic garden!

He saw pink and white petals belonging to the dog roses, arched and scrambling in hedgerow, and there were orchids and huge daisies everywhere. The winding, narrow path that found them under an iron archway was filled with the strongest smell of jasmine he had ever encountered. With one single intake of his breath, he took the aroma with him. They approached the back of an old fashioned, yet charming, little courtyard where a large cypress tree was giving shelter to some boys sitting beneath it.

This was it.... this is where his new life was to begin.

It was four a.m. - pitch black outside, and the sun had not yet risen when little Harry awoke. If only he could have known that the peacefulness he was feeling right then would soon be over, as his day was about to begin at the hands of the dreaded Mr Sava. He'd heard from the other boys about the daily beatings, so if he was to avoid turning black and blue, he was to do as he was told because there would be no mercy - make no mistake of that - for whatever got in Mr Sava's way, got crushed. Harry was there to learn a trade, and he was a hard worker, but that made no difference to the evil Mr Sava, as far as he was concerned, he was doing him a favour, which meant he had to be grateful - show gratitude for having been given a roof over his head, a meal and a bed, but the price for such luxuries was high for a poor boy that came from a small village far from here. Half asleep and starving, his first job was to clean out the muck at Mr Sava's dairy farm and when that was done he would brush and groom the cows getting them ready for milking. He then fed the chickens, collected their freshly laid eggs and walked the two miles to the local grocery shop to sell them. Then, after all was done at the farm he would clean the main house from top to bottom, wash the dishes and mop the floors. Only when his morning chores were finished could he have his breakfast and get ready for work in the city-centre, where Mr Sava was building a house for a wealthy businessman.

As soon as he got there, Harry would start by rendering the walls with plaster, making sure to cover them thinly and flat the way Mr

Easter, April 1977, England.

Sava had shown him - or there would be trouble. On one particular morning, Harry had woken up, as usual, at the crack of dawn, done his chores to perfection and made his way to the wealthy mans' house, but on this particular day, Mr Sava was vexed and out of control; out to draw blood. He repeatedly found fault in everything Harry was doing, then finally losing it, he took hold of a large stick and laid into him, lashing at him like a madman. Harry dared not to cry, not even to make a sound if he wanted Mr Sava to stop.

When that part of his terrifying day had finished, he made his way back home, black and blue with a dull, aching pain all over, only to be confronted by Mr Sava's daughter, Maroulla as she sat enjoying the company of some girlfriends in the garden. Embarrassed of how filthy he must have looked, he hurriedly walked passed them only to be called back.

'Wait! Come here! Are you Harry Constantine?' Laughed Maroulla.

He stopped and without turning around to look at her, replied a straight, 'yes.'

'Well look at me when I am speaking to you.'

Refusing to do as he was told, especially by a girl, he stood there with his back to her.

'What do you want?' He asked.

'I'm thirsty, fetch me some water.'

'Get it yourself.'

'I said fetch me a glass of water Harry Constantine.'

'No.'

Then without warning, she got up and took to him with a broom. He turned around and grabbed hold of it making her struggle, swinging her from side to side, half playing and half teasing as they fought like brother and sister, and with one tug he flung her to the ground.

'I'm going to tell my papa,' she threatened.

'Tell him,' he said, dropping the broom at her feet.

'I will!'

But she never did, because if she had, she knew he would have had the beating of his life, and although she'd witnessed her papa's violent beatings of the boys, seen the lives he'd destroyed, she felt an admiration for Harry, for his spirit was never dampened.

*   *   *   *   *   *   *   *   *

52

Easter, April 1977, England.

Holding Megan in my arms, my cry turned into a sob, I felt such a mixture of emotions towards my papa, some of love and some of fear. Fearing his rejection, I was scared of voicing my opinion without his approval - because I always feared he'd perhaps stop loving me if I dared to be different. The problem was, I was different and I hated to disappoint him because I loved him, I loved him very much.

My birthday had started as one of the best days ever, but had sadly ended in tears. I thought of Jonathan, the scared look that had appeared on his face when he saw papa standing in my room and how awful he must be feeling right now. That's when I began sobbing like I'd never sobbed before, in a kind of self pity, knowing that whatever I felt I must put aside and pull myself together, go downstairs and face everyone as if nothing had happened. So I forced myself to sit up, wiping away my tears. I kept hold of Megan and made my way down.

'Where have you been my sweet child?' Said mama standing halfway up the stairs, 'I've been looking all over for you.'

'I was in my room mama.' I replied, hoping she wouldn't notice I'd been crying.

'Oh, my little daydreamer,' she said, holding out her hand. 'Now let's put her in the sitting room with the other dolls. Everybody's waiting to sing happy birthday to you.'

So with a dampened spirit, I reluctantly handed Megan over to her.

When we returned to the garden, we were greeted with cheers. Papa was holding a huge pink cake that was ablaze with fifteen pink and white candles, and as if nothing had happened, I put on my smile.

'*Happy Birthday to you,*' he began to sing. '*Happy Birthday to you,*' everyone joined in. '*Happy birthday dear Sofia . . . . . . Happy Birthday to you.*'

Then without daring to look Jonathan's way, I blew out my candles and made a wish!

Summer, July 1977, England.

Chapter Six

'Yes! Yes Freda darling, yes it's true! We are all coming to Cyprus. Every one of us!'

I could hear mama, she was shouting down the telephone. 'Call it Harry's belated fortieth birthday party darling and tell Kosta not to make up the beds. We still have four weeks to go!' She was shouting even louder now.

'I too will be counting the days...Freda! Freda darling! I can't hear you!'

Auntie Freda's voice had become so faint; mama had no choice but to hang up the receiver. She tried the number again and again but it was no good, the line was dead! It was most inconvenient, when calling Auntie Freda in Cyprus, because she didn't have a telephone in her house, no one did. There was only one in the entire village and that was in the small café where the men used to gather to play cards and backgammon drinking Cypriot coffee for hours as they watched the world drift by. It certainly wasn't a place where women would be welcome.

A young boy working at the café would run to my Auntie Freda's house whenever we phoned, to let her know she had a long distance call. Poor Auntie Freda would then have to drop whatever she was doing and take to the road, running as fast as her legs could carry her.

'Mama,' I said, walking into the living room. I sat down beside her but she didn't hear me, she didn't even know I was there; she was gazing into the garden, staring into space. I looked over at the summerhouse but papa and Aunt Demi came into my mind so I quickly turned away.

'Mama,' I said again, softly this time so that I wouldn't alarm her. She gave her head a gentle shake and then she looked at me with a confused, almost blank, expression on her face. 'Sorry Sofia, I was miles away.'

'That's okay, mama. I just wanted to know what time we were leaving.

'Leaving?'

54

Summer, July 1977, England.

'Yes.'

'Well, I'm not sure. Why? Where are we going?'

'To *yia'ya's.*'

'Why? What's happened?!'

'Nothing. She'll be worried if we're late.'

'Late for what Sofia?'

'It's Friday mama. We go to *yia'ya's* on Friday.'

'Oh, of course we do, how silly of me to forget.'

'So shall we get ready now mama?'

'Yes. Yes, get ready and tell Christina and Irini to get ready too,' she replied, looking a little embarrassed, probably wondering what I was thinking of her forgetfulness.

'Okay. I'll do it now.'

I gave her a smile, just to reassure her that I didn't think anything of her lack of memory, hoping it wasn't because her mind was busy with ideas about papa and Aunt Demi. I got up to walk away but she took hold of my hand.

'You're a good girl, Sofia, and I love you, very much,' she sighed, reaching up to give me a kiss.

I could only look down and smile at her, desperately hoping she never found out about papa and Aunt Demi; I loved her so much and I knew it would finish her if she ever did.

I rose up her hand and kissed it. 'I love you too mama,' I replied, fighting to keep the tears back.

'Now you run along, my sweet girl,' she smiled, her head slowly turning towards the garden again. 'Now go and get ready before *yia'ya* starts to worry.' And as she let go of her tight grasp, I turned around and ran to find Christina and Irini.

I absolutely loved Fridays, not only because it meant we had finished another week of school but because that was the day we visited my *yia'ya* Athena's. Mama allowed us to stay over some weekends when we didn't have too much homework; this was one of those weekends.

As soon as we'd got there, the first thing we did was unpack. We would hang our clothes in the wardrobe and lay out our pyjamas neatly on the huge double bed where all three of us slept together. I always took a moment by myself to say hello to *bapou* Christos; there

Summer, July 1977, England.

was an old black and white photo of him and my *yia'ya* on the little dressing table where we placed our board games and books.

Taken on the day they got married, he looked very smart in his wedding suit. I'd not ever seen a Greek man dressed that way, in traditional costume, but in Cyprus it was still very common to see old men wearing the *vra'ka*; a funny, baggy looking trouser that stopped at the knee. *Bapou's* sash, we were told, was tied around the groom's waist during the wedding ceremony to symbolize their union and his striped silk shirt was given to him by *yia'ya*, a gift from the bride-to-be. My *yia'ya* was so young when they got married, just sixteen and he was only nineteen but they looked a lot older, they looked ancient!

I sat looking intently at the photo, trying to connect with *bapou*, trying so hard to remember what he was like or something we did together, but I couldn't think of very much. I was nine years old when he passed away.

Christina and Irini left me alone sitting on the bed holding *bapou's* photo and it took me back to another Friday. I smiled to myself remembering when we'd come to visit *yia'ya* only to be greeted by the cutest, fluffiest, little white dog I had ever laid eyes on, a West Highland Terrier named Will, but I liked calling him William because he looked very royal and extremely important.

Mama didn't feel the same way about William as I did because she'd been bitten by a dog when she was a small girl in Cyprus and the presence of them used to make her run with fear. Unfortunately, she had embedded her fears within us too, but William seemed harmless; all he wanted was to play, so I sat down on the floor, on my knees, and introduced myself to him.

'*Bapou*, what's his name?' I asked.

'Will....short for William. Do you like him Sofia? He's a Westy, a pedigree I believe.'

'Hello William, I'm Sofia. Glad to make your acquaintance,' I said, shaking his tiny paw.

'Oh, I think he likes you,' laughed *bapou*, as William began licking my hand.

'He's so cute. Can we take him to the park in the morning *bapou*?' I asked laughing. I couldn't take my eyes off him.

'Sure we can and you can hold his lead.'

56

Summer, July 1977, England.

'Can I *bapou*?! Can I?!' I said excitedly.

To anybody else a simple act like taking a dog to the park may not have been thrilling, just a chore, but for me it had been one of many great days I experienced as a young girl when I could get away from rules and rigid Greek traditions.

The next day we got up extra early, had breakfast and left, just *bapou*, William and me. When we got to the park, *bapou* handed me the lead and we were off straight away; unexpectedly for me but not for William, he'd done this many times before. So running like crazy, he pulled me across the huge green, my feet hardly touching the ground as he dragged me around every tree and back again, and the further we went the further *bapou* got, 'til he turned into a dot, almost becoming invisible in the distance. I held on to the lead so tightly not wanting to let go, not wanting to lose William, and when our marathon was over, we returned to *bapou*, exhilarated.

I would have given anything to relive that day, even if it was the once, anything to be with *bapou* and William again.

However, my happy thoughts were gradually beginning to fade as *bapou* was now taking me back to one summer afternoon at *Holly Blue* when I was playing out in our front garden with Emma, my first china doll.

I'd sat Emma down with my teddies on a bench pretending they were at my tearoom and that I was serving them my best cream cakes. I hadn't meant to break the china tea set *bapou* had bought for me, but as I turned to run and greet him, that's how it happened, that's when it all fell to the ground, smashing into a hundred pieces. I cried and cried because I'd been so clumsy, and I was so very sorry. All he could do was comfort me, promising he'd buy me another, but he never did because a few weeks later he had the accident and died. It was terrible because that's all I could think about on the day of his funeral - that I'd broken my lovely tea set - my precious gift from him.

As the tears welled up in my eyes, I knew it was time for me to go downstairs, so I kissed *bapou's* photo, put it back on the dressing table and left with my memories. Returning to the kitchen there was a wonderful smell of burning toast where my *yia'ya* was preparing an early evening feast for us of thickly cut Greek bread, which she sliced and grilled to perfection, garlic salami, *haloumi* cheese and green cracked garlic olives, all served with fresh tomatoes and cucumber. We filled our plates and sat at the table in the back room overlooking the garden. It looked nothing like the one we'd spent Guy Fawkes Day in last November, when every tree was bare, without a flower in sight, unlike now, everything was in full bloom.

The beautiful sea of colour was so strong it was almost blinding to the naked eye, and amongst all the fantastic flowers, she had grown, her enormous dahlias were the most impressive. They were magnificent, her pride and joy! She took care of them with so much love and patience they seemed to grow larger by the minute, leaving her equally green-fingered neighbours bewildered and baffled as to how she did it. *Yia'ya* would spend hours pruning and snipping, digging and planting, becoming somewhat of a professional gardener. It was the only thing that kept her going since losing *bapou*.

'Your dahlias are gigantic this year Mrs Michalli. The biggest I've ever seen them,' observed mama. She called her '*Mrs Michalli*' sometimes when they where joking around.

'Oh don't let my neighbours hear you praising my dahlias Elena, I'm the talk of the street, and the envy. But I do think it's the ants we should be thanking this year.'

'Why the ants?' Asked mama, looking at her a little puzzled.

'Well have you not seen my wonderful giant daisies?'

'Where?' She said, getting up and going over to the window to get a closer look. She turned her head from left to right. 'Oh yes, I can see them. But what have the ants done now?'

'Nothing other than carry daisy seeds into my garden when Mrs Fletcher, next door, had refused to part with some,' she replied, laughing quietly to herself.

Laughing with her, she said, 'Oh *Mrs Michalli*! You're so full of tricks!'

We weren't altogether convinced the ants had really carried the daisy seeds over to *yia'ya's* garden, though we would never let her know....but one thing was for sure, only my *yia'ya* could have said for something like that to happen. And whether or not it was the work of the ants, the daisies were there and standing tall!

By the time we'd finished eating, it was soon time for us to make our way up to our room. It wasn't late, but mama didn't like us going to bed after ten o'clock, and by time we read some books and played 'Monopoly', my favourite board game, we would hardly be able to keep our eyes open anyway.

The next morning, I was impolitely woken at the crack of dawn by a loud knock on the letter box and a high pitched yelp. It was far too early, and the sun had not yet risen, but Fred was making his morning delivery. Tall and extremely thin, he looked more like a scrawny scarecrow than a milkman. Christina and I used to make up stories about him, scaring the boys and girls who lived on *yia'ya's* street half silly. It still put a huge smile on my face whenever I thought back to the day we sat them all down in *yia'ya's* front garden one late afternoon to tell them about Fred the milkman. I suppose we had papa's sense of humour - him with the snails, us with Fred!

I could still see Christina as she began - putting on her best story telling voice.

'Once upon a time in a far away place, that no one had ever heard of, stood a happy, new scarecrow called Fred who was once loved and wanted very much, but, as time went by, the happy, new scarecrow became sad and old, and because he had become slow and couldn't chase away the birds anymore, the farmer couldn't keep him, so he threw him on the rubbish heap to be taken away. The sad and old scarecrow waited until the farmer had gone to bed, got down from the heap, then walked one hundred miles to the city. It was such a long way away that by the time he'd got there it was nearly Christmas, and because Fred had lost all faith in the farmer that had once been his friend, he became miserable and bitter, roaming the streets of London in his tatty clothes on Christmas Eve, turning off Christmas lights everywhere.' They listened with their eyes wide open as I took the story over to tell them more.

A little ginger haired boy called Trevor, who lived four doors away with his mum Wendy, screamed every time we told them that story, and would run home in floods of tears, only returning to play once he'd recovered from the trauma.

'Can I have a ride on your bike Trevor?' I asked, one day.

'Only if you and Christina never tell us about Fred and the Christmas lights, ever again,' he said, wiping his snotty little nose on

Summer, July 1977, England.

the back of his sleeve.

'Yes, okay.'

'Promise?'

'Only if you let me ride your bike? Is that a yes?'

He took a long look at me wondering if I was telling him the truth and pushing up his little round spectacles replied: 'Yes.'

'Thanks, Trevor, see you in a minute,' I said, taking hold of the handlebars. And I was off!

My papa never allowed us to have a bike, and I couldn't remember why, but he'd said; *'Bikes were only for boys.'* adding sternly; *'They were forbidden in Cyprus for young ladies.'* But we weren't in Cyprus now, we were in England, Trevor had lent me his bike and I was going to ride it and papa would never know.

This was the best part of my summer holiday; playing outside with the boys and girls on *yia'ya's* street. Our Turkish friends, the twins Murat and Shiver moved here around the time my *bapou* Christos had died. Always the first ones out, they would gulp down their supper as quickly as possible not wanting to waste a single moment of valuable playing time.

One early evening when we were out playing, Shiver had been kicking a football about with the boys when she ran across the road to get the ball and hadn't seen the London black cab until it hit her. She was as tough as old boots though, because she just picked herself up and continued to run. When her mum found out, she ran from the house screaming, grabbed hold of Shiver and dragged her home by the ear, and if getting knocked over wasn't enough, she was smacking her as well!

Murat was so oblivious to his mum's reaction, because that's the way she dealt with everything, a pulling of the ear and a smack on the back of the legs. So before Shiver was dragged off he just snatched the ball off her and continued his game.

I remember thinking how alike we all were; even though we came from different backgrounds and practiced different religions. My papa also always over-reacted to everything, as did the twins' mum. Within half an hour all had been forgotten and Shiver had returned outside.

60

She always loved to play '*What's the time Mr Wolf?*' but I preferred '*Knock down Ginger,*' a game where we picked a house, knocked on the front door then ran and hid. We would wait with excitement for the poor victim to open their door. I loved it! We used to pick on the same houses repeatedly, watching as their owners became more and more annoyed, and the more annoyed they got, the more we did it.

Our favourite '*Knock down Ginger*' was when we repeatedly knocked on the door of a spiteful old lady called Mrs Skinner who lived all alone with her three black cats. Whenever our ball went over her fence she would take it into her house, never to be seen again. I was convinced she was a witch, because only witches had three black cats, a long pointy nose, big wide feet and enormous hair that looked like a scraggly old birds nest. She would open her door, walk slowly to her front gate, look around to see if she could see us and then go back inside, but just as she was about to close the door behind her, she would quickly open it again in order to catch us out, but to her alarm she never did. We must have knocked on her door ten times before she gave up; finding it so funny that we laughed until our stomachs hurt and our jaws ached.

My dear friends Paris and Desy were always the last out; their mama was not well and needed help around the house. She'd been ill for as long as I could remember and very rarely went out, and because I didn't understand what was wrong with her I was always frightened when I went round to call. I remember the day she invited me in to meet Jenny. I rang the bell and waited, hoping Paris or Desy would open the door.

'Hello. Sofia is it?'

'Hello Mrs Bandelli,' I replied nervously, hoping she wouldn't ask me in.

'You like come in, Paris and Desy not be long.' She spoke English with a heavy Greek accent, and not very well.

'No, it's okay Mrs Bandelli. I'll wait here.'

'Come! Say hello to Jenny.'

'Jenny?'

'My canary.'

'Oh, okay.'

She showed me in and I followed her to the back of the house to a

61

room where she spent most of her time sitting embroidering and where she kept her beloved birds. It was filled with the finest, most beautifully finished tapestries, they were everywhere, all of them of birds, all different types and of every species, and they must have taken her years to do.

'These are lovely Mrs Bandelli,' I said, looking around at them all.

'It is shame I have not time to frame them? Yes?' She said, as she opened the door of the bird cage where Jenny sat. She took her out and gave her to me.

'Oh Mrs Bandelli she's so tiny, she looks just like a tiny yellow cotton wool ball.'

'Yes, but she has big heart and when she sings…*well* the whole street hear her.'

'Mama, we've finished tidying up. Can we go out now?' Asked Paris, as she entered the room with Desy.

'I show Jenny to Sofia,' she said, ignoring the question.

'Would you like us to do anything else mama?' Asked Desy.

'I telling Sofia the whole street hear her when she sings.'

'Yes Mama. Is it okay then, can we go out?' Paris asked again.

'Of course, you run go and sure to come home not late? Yes?'

'Okay mama.'

'Nice to seeing you Sofia!' She called. 'Come again and please tell hello to your *yia'ya* for me? Yes?'

'I will, Mrs Bandelli. Bye!' I called back, as we closed the front door.

This was how we spent our summer holidays at *yia'ya's*, playing in the street without a care in the world and with our friends from all walks of life.

Summer, August 1977 Cyprus.

Chapter Seven

I t was to become one of the hottest summers ever, from the moment we stepped off the plane, the dry, burning heat from the sun hit my face and I quickly put on my huge yellow straw hat, reminding me of what was to come. Dressed only in a short daisy print cotton dress, it didn't take long for it to start sticking to me, becoming very uncomfortable and itchy. I could see the minibuses waiting on the tarmac ready to take us into Larnaca Airport's baggage lounge where we would be collecting our cases. I didn't know which was worse, walking from the plane feeling as though I'd stepped into an inferno or getting on a bus that was as hot as an oven, or then having to sit on the scorching plastic seat; it was horrible!

Once the buses were near enough to the airport, we got down and walked some more until we eventually entered an air-conditioned lounge. The women stood with the children, watching as the men battled with the cases. One by one they fought with them as they went round and around on the conveyor belt. They all looked the same to me, but papa seemed to have worked out which ones were ours.

I sat on a hard plastic chair cuddling up to *yia'ya* Athena, tired and thirsty but keeping my moans and complaints to myself. Finally, when the cases had all arrived, papa and my Uncles, Mike, George and Nick put them all on trolleys and we were off. When we got outside, we were greeted by my larger than life Uncle Kosta and papa's cousins, my Uncle Dagi and Uncle Alex. It was at least half an hour before we loaded the cases into the cars, got in and left the airport, because that's how long it took for everyone to kiss and say hello.

'Forrrr... you, Sofia,' said my Uncle Kosta, giving me a bracelet he'd made out of jasmine.

'Thank you, Uncle Kosta, it smells lovely,' I said, putting it to my nose.

'And one for You... and for You... and for You... and for You,' he said, handing one each to Christina, Irini and my cousins Helen and

63

little Anna. 'You're my five little princesses from England. Oh and let us not forget our baby Elizabeth… and one for you!' He laughed.

'Thank you, Uncle Kosta,' we echoed.

'Say thank you Uncle Kosta,' mama said to Elizabeth.

But Elizabeth couldn't pronounce his name and thanked her Uncle 'Dosta.'

We all laughed at Elizabeth clapping her hands repeating his name.

'Now come my little princesses, come everyone, let us get into the cars. Let us go to the village where your Auntie Freda and *yia'ya* Elizabeth are waiting.'

It had been a long four years since we'd all visited our Mother Land, Cyprus, all of us together like this but it seemed as though time had stood still and nothing had changed. It was all as I'd remembered it to be the first time we'd visited this little paradise island. Miles and miles of creamy-yellow, dry flat land blended with handsome Mediterranean cypress trees growing on volcanic looking hills, extremely different to the green pastures of England. It wasn't a long drive to the place we called our second home; however, by the time we got to Auntie Freda's we were very tired, very hungry and very hot! When we finally got there, the village was also just as I'd remembered it. Totou, as it was called, was about a fifteen-minute drive from the city of Paphos.

Papa had told us Paphos was one of the oldest cities in Cyprus and was once the capital. Built during the twelfth and thirteenth centuries B.C., Achaean Greeks came to settle on the island bringing with them the Greek language, their religion and their customs. The whole region was spectacular, a place where Aphrodite, the Greek goddess of love and beauty was born. It was a myth that had lived on through the ages and believed by romantic lovers worldwide. And just as I'd thought of the historical stories papa used to tell us, I caught sight of *Petra Tou Romiou*, the frothy waves splashing on it, just as they had for thousands of years before us. It all felt so romantic.

Totou, a small village compared to others in the area, was hidden in the mountains with only a narrow dirt track for a road leading to it. Built on a drop, it was quite terrifying to get to and all I could do was hold on to Christina for dear life as we went round and around, higher

Summer, August 1977 Cyprus.

and higher, the drop becoming steeper and steeper.

If the plane flight and the heat from the inferno didn't kill us, I was sure these mountains would! I buried my face into Christina's arm waiting to die; I shut my eyes and just waited.

'Sofia! Sofia! We're here, its okay. We're here!' She screeched, reassuringly.

I managed to pull myself away and as I slowly opened my eyes I could see the little village with its little houses, its crooked streets and narrow pavements. I was alive!

Suddenly the bells of St John's rang, it was Sunday and there was a wedding. I quickly turned to catch a glimpse of the beautiful bride as she was running with her handsome groom. He kissed her to a cheering crowd as she threw them her bouquet; I gave a hearty sigh as Jonathan entered my mind.

We must have looked so important to the people of this small village, stepping out of a fleet of cars. I don't think many of them had ever been anywhere else in their entire lives; that's where they were born, went to school and got married, for most of them that's where they lived until they died. It was a simple life, nothing complicated and not much expected.

The young girls did as their *mitera's* had done before them, as long as they made their families proud and married a local boy, everybody would be happy - or that's what they were led to believe.

An arranged meeting of two families by a mutual friend was still the only form of getting married. The arrangement, or *brox'en'yia* as it was called, was still widely practiced. The father of one family would ask a mediator to introduce his son to the daughter of another family. It was a tradition used for hundreds of years in Cyprus, a tradition that allowed one family to be united with another, bringing together the perfect match! The problem was, if two families wanted to merge, the *brox'en'yia* would sometimes be agreed without little consideration for the bride and groom's wishes.

This wasn't quite the case with my mama and papa though, their meeting had been arranged by a mutual friend, and my papa himself had asked his friend to be the mediator. For as we'd all been told on a million occasions, he'd fallen in love with mama when they were both still at school and had wanted her as his bride from the moment he'd

Summer, August 1977 Cyprus.

laid eyes on her.

'Freda! Freda Come! Look who I have brought to see you!' Called out Uncle Kosta as we started emerging from the cars outside their house.

Auntie Freda ran from the house screaming our names, one after the other, waving her arms in the air and crying. She embraced as all at once, not knowing who to go for first, kissing us whilst studying our faces.

'Oh, my lovely babies, you grown so big,' she cried, tears streaming down her face.

My mama and papa were now crying too, which started my *yia'ya* Athena, then my Aunties, in fact, they all joined in, and even my Uncles were fighting back the tears. This trip had been long awaited.

'Come my little ones, *yia'ya* Elizabeth not sleeps all night waiting for you,' she said in her broken English, wiping her eyes on her apron, ushering us towards the back of their house.

She led us down a cobble-stoned pathway towards barns where a few cows were poking out their heads; the stench was so strong it almost suffocated me. I quickly put my hand up to my nose, squeezing it tightly, but the smell, bitter and strong, still managed to linger through, so grabbing hold of Christina and Irini, I began to run fearing I might faint if we walked any slower. The chickens that were roaming freely around the yard, pecking at the odd corn here and there, must have thought we had come for them and they panicked, running for their lives - reminding me of the crazy days we spent with the ones over the fence at the bottom of our garden.

Yia'ya Elizabeth stepped out of her tiny house to see why the chickens were in such a confusion and that's when we ran straight into her arms. She automatically bent down to greet us and I thought how different she looked, and smelt, compared to *yia'ya* Athena. She was tall and slim with a distinctive out of doors smell, it wasn't horrid, just a smell of nature and the warmth of the sun, whereas *yia'ya* Athena was short and a little plump and always smelt of a rosy perfume. I could see my sister Irini in *yia'ya* Elizabeth, she resembled her so much, and I imagined that's how she would look in years to come. I just wanted to wrap her up and take her back home with us to England; she looked almost unreal, as if she were one of those Greek dolls I noticed in the window of the souvenir shop at the airport - dressed in traditional costume, a one-piece waisted and pleated dress,

Summer, August 1977 Cyprus.

a *fou'stani*, which was the preferred over-garment in rural areas of Cyprus and particularly in the mountains.

'Pedri! Pedri!' She called out to him, 'look Pedri our princesses!' Except, sadly my *bapou* Pedri had also passed away, as had my *bapou* Christos. I liked to think of them somewhere nice together where all they did all day was play backgammon, drink Cypriot coffee and go on long walks in the park with William.

The rest of the day was spent chatting and catching up on events of the past four years and in between chatting there was crying - a lot of crying - and it all began to get a bit too much for me, so I took to the road by myself on this warm night in order to clear my head. There were no worries for my safety for everybody in the village was more or less related, and if by any chance they weren't they all knew each other well. It felt so surreal walking through the village where most of the adults in my family had been born. It was as if no other place in the world existed, like it was a place no one knew or could imagine, and I was really overwhelmed by it all, just the idea that this was my family's birth place brought tears of joy to my eyes. I was truly in love with it, in love with it's cow-filled smelly barns, its chickens running like crazy in their yards and in love with the herds of sheep with their tiny brass bells rattling as they roamed on the dry mountains with their shepherds.

I looked up at the blackened night, and the stars looked truly amazing, twinkling like a million fairy lights, then out of the blue Jonathan popped into my thoughts again; wondering if he was staring at them from his bedroom window and whether they looked the same to him. I took in a deep breath, and along with my sigh I smelt the strong sweet fragrance of jasmine that was so characteristic of this beautiful island.

'*Kali'spera*,' said an old man, as he tried to straighten himself up with support from his equally old walking stick. He looked straight at me but I could see he hadn't recognised me.

'Oh, good evening, and *kali'spera* to you. I'm Sofia,' I introduced myself to him.

'I am Elena's daughter.'

'Elena?'

'Yes,' I replied, nodding my head.

67

'Sofia? Sofia?' He repeated. '*Dada* Dimitri.' He pointed at himself with his long, crocked fingers.

'*Bapou* Dimitri?'

'*Dada*,' he corrected me.

'*Dada* Dimitri?'

'*Nai*,' he agreed, nodding his head.

'Oh yes,' I remembered. Mama told us about her godfather, Dimitri Stefanou, her *dada*. He was my *bapou* Christos closest friend and best man at their wedding - who then went on to become my mama's godfather - the greatest honour one Greek can give to another.

He was in front of me, looking as though he'd just stepped out of a photo from one of the albums *yia'ya* Athena had back home in England - still wearing his *vraka*, just like the one *bapou* Christos had on in the photo that sat on *yia'ya's* dressing table - maybe that's how *bapou* would have dressed if he hadn't emigrated to England, I thought.

I smiled at him politely and taking hold of his hand, I kissed the back of it, a custom papa taught us to do to old people in order to show our respect. He raised his walking stick, giving a shaky wave, '*goodbye*.'

I carried on my walk through this ancient little village, '*kali'spera*,' waved a cheery lady standing on her porch, watering her flowers while her husband relaxed with a glass of ouzo watching television.

'*Kali'spera*,' I waved back, letting my silent walk take me further to the little café where my Auntie Freda would run to when we called from England. It was all beginning to feel extremely bizarre - the village, *dada* Dimitri and now the café! I felt the goose-bumps tingling my skin as the night drew in and looking down at my watch I decided to make my way back to Auntie Freda's. First I wanted to say goodnight to *yia'ya* Elizabeth so I went by a short cut that led me to the back yard and traced my way down the cobbled pathway in the direction of the building *yia'ya* called her home. I noticed a light still on so I knocked on the door and entered only to find her sitting on her bed wearing a long creamy nightshirt and bloomers, plaiting her long silver-white hair. That was probably the only time her hair would be on show, when she combed and plaited it at night and in the mornings.

'Hello *yia'ya* - *yasou*,' I smiled, correcting myself.

'*Yasou* Sofia.'

I sat down beside her and watched as she parted her hair in the

Summer, August 1977 Cyprus.

middle, plaiting it into two long braids. Only old women, widows and those in mourning wore a black 'kerchief I was told and the *kouroukla*, as it was called in Greek, covered the hair, forehead and ears like a snood and was known as the *skoufoma*.

She continued plaiting, showing me how it was done, telling me in her own words that this was how I would plait my beautiful hair when I became an old lady like her. When she finished, she twisted the two long braids at the top of her head.

'Yes, maybe I will plait my hair like that,' I said to her in English. She knew what I meant, I didn't need to say it in Greek, I just smiled lovingly at this woman I'd heard so much about but had spent such little time with during my life growing up in England. I sat watching her as she stood up and walked over to the tiny window, she pulled shut the wooden shutters and then dimmed the little oil lamp on the table by her bed. It all looked very primitive compared to my bedroom back in England, where I had thick expensive carpet lining the floor and heavy fringed curtains at my window.

'What my two girls doing?' Said Auntie Freda, as she entered the room, something she did every night, checking to see if *yia'ya* was alright before going to bed herself.

'*Yia'ya* showed me how she plaits her hair. Isn't it lovely?'

'Yes, it is. The old girl still beautiful,' she laughed, stroking the top of *yia'ya's* head as she kissed her goodnight. 'Your papa is to take you all to thala'sa in the morning Sofia, say *Kali'nih'ta* to *yia'ya*,' she smiled, as she pulled back *yia'ya's* bed sheets.

I kissed *yia'ya's* bony cheek and left.

*   *   *   *   *   *   *   *   *

While the village was coming back to life, with sounds that weren't familiar to me, I could hear the cockerel singing his early morning song, cows in their sheds mooing after having been rid of the milk in their heavy udders and goats rattling the brass bells that hung from their necks as they ran in the distant field. I tried to block them out as I tossed and turned in my bed. Wondering if I should get up, I glanced over at Christina from beneath my sheet and noticed she was still sleeping, but there was no sign of Irini. Never one for having a lie in, she was always eager to make an early start to her day. I, on the other hand, was not a morning girl - not even on such lovely days as these. Mama would be calling for us to be ready soon enough, so I just took advantage of my laziness for a little bit more as the cool mountain breeze entered the room. I closed my eyes and began daydreaming about Jonathan and a huge grin appeared across my face.

Suddenly I was shaken back to reality by a gigantic bang, which sounded like an exhaust pipe exploding directly in front of the house. I threw back my sheet and ran to the window pulling back the net curtains to see what it was, but I couldn't quite make out what was happening, it seemed as though all the women of the entire village were huddled around one little white van and one solitary man. He was showing them sheets and sheets and blankets - bundles of blankets and bath towels, bath towels and more bath towels - every colour, every size! They were all buying them like there was no tomorrow. With an inquisitive mind such as mine, I was finding the whole thing so fascinating that I wanted to get a closer look, so I immediately put on my dressing gown and ran downstairs. When my Auntie Freda caught sight of me, she looked horrified because I was still in my nightclothes.

'Sofia! No my little one, you come outside half dressed? No! Not in front of man! Get inside now.' she said, shielding me from the salesman.

'But auntie I don't want to. I want to see what's going on,' I protested.

'No Sofia....now!' She said firmly, pointing her finger to the front door.

Only when all the mayhem had come to an end and my auntie had finished buying everything she could lay her hands on could I pull myself away from the window where I'd stood and watched.

I suppose it was a kind of Greek version of what mama called, 'retail therapy'. I could see her now making her way towards the house, her singing getting louder the closer she got. So quickly running upstairs before she caught sight of me, I jumped straight back into bed and pulled the sheet over my head. Her singing was getting even louder as she walked up the stairs, kicking off her flip-flops and entering our room going straight to the wardrobe where she neatly placed the

Summer, August 1977 Cyprus.

mountain of sheets, pillowcases and towels, I pretended to be asleep.

She'd told us a long time ago how she'd been collecting them over the years to give to us as part of our dowry when we got married. It wasn't something all aunties did but she didn't have children of her own so she looked upon us girls as her own daughters.

'Get dressed Sofia. You come for walk with me?' She asked, looking over from the wardrobe.

'Where are we going auntie?' I yawned, stretching out my arms.

'You will see. It is fun. We going to *foon'dana*, to collect water, you meet other aunties there,' she replied, walking out of the room.

'Christina get up. Let's go with Auntie Freda to collect some water.'

'Where from?' She asked in a sleepy voice.

'I'm not sure. The *foon'dana?*'

'No. Go with Irini.'

'Please Christina. I'm not going by myself. Irini won't want to come.'

'No,' she said again, only this time turning her back to me.

'Christina. Please? Please?'

'Okay, okay,' she grunted, waving me away as if to say, 'be quiet'.

'Come on it'll be fun. Get dressed.'

When we got downstairs, Auntie Freda was waiting for us holding some buckets. It was something she and all the other young women did every day; collecting water from a tap in the middle of the village - the *foon'dana* -a place where they would meet to catch up on the latest gossip on who was marrying whom.

We took a bucket and followed her. It was hard work living life in a small village, Auntie Freda's day started at the crack of dawn. She would first milk the cows, feed the chickens, collect their eggs to sell and then she would clean the house from top to bottom, as papa had done many years ago and even though the life he led was now a million miles away, it was still very real for the people of this island.

How spoilt we were - us with our buckets going to collect water - treating it as an adventure, just killing time before we set off on a fun filled day at the beach. We didn't have a clue what hard work was all about but we were soon to find out. When we got there Auntie Freda introduced us to each and every one of the women. First to make our acquaintance was Kyriakoulla, she was about the same age as Irini, but already the effects of the sun had aged her skin which made her look a lot older. Kyriakoulla had left school and was working from home where she helped her mama cover heels for a large shoe factory in Paphos. I can still remember noticing her grubby hands and feet and how sad that made me feel, for here she was covering heels for mere pennies, and probably only owned one pair of shoes herself, which, no doubt, she wore on Sundays when she went to church.

Her sister, Fanoulla, was a little shabby but a very beautiful girl. She stood close to her mama not saying much, just filling bucket after bucket with no emotion on her face. She was not much older than me, yet she lacked confidence and her insecurities from being mocked about her weight seemed to haunt her openly. Her family knew it would be difficult to find her a suitable husband - sadly, she knew her prince would never come!

Taking hold of her hand, I introduced myself, hoping to get a response, though alas, it was her mama's voice that answered me. Fanoulla just smiled sheepishly through her long curly locks but I felt her tightening grip silently welcoming the unfamiliar attention she was receiving. The blazing sun gradually rose higher in the bright sky, telling us the heat would be getting hotter and soon it would time for the mid morning siesta allowing us to make our way back home for our outing with papa.

He drove us south along the coast from Paphos to *Petra Tou Romiou*, reminding us once again that it was the birth place of Aphrodite, where, surprisingly it was not overly crowded. Finding a great place on the beach where we could sit privately and uninterrupted, day after day we visited the same spot, until it became so familiar the adults became quite comfortable about dropping us kids off there when they had something else planned. However, every time we were dropped off, Aunt Demi would quickly jump out of her car and get into ours, any excuse being with my papa. I hated it, the very thought of her in our car with my mama there too made my stomach turn. Even on the days they stayed with us at the beach didn't make a difference to my feeling. Aunt Demi and Uncle Mike would go for long walks along the coast, always inviting papa to join them. It wasn't enough they were carrying on with this affair back home in England, they couldn't

Summer, August 1977 Cyprus.

keep away from each other even on our summer holiday. They were becoming pathetically boring with their constant flirting. And today she hadn't even waited for us to get dropped off. I sat squashed between her and Christina staring out at the ocean my thoughts wandering back to the day the adults wanted to go up to Troodos Mountains. That was the day we met our cousin Andreas and his two brothers, Stavros and Manoli. They too were at the beach because their parents had arranged to meet up with ours.

We had been dropped off at our usual spot with plenty of food and drink, but it was almost as if we were the only ones there that day, apart from a few Greek boys playing ball in the sea and a couple of girls out for a successful day of sun bathing. My boisterous cousins were busy showing off, splashing around and making as much noise as they could, desperately trying to get the attention of the girls' sun bathing. Christina and Irini were in the warm, clear sea with Helen and little Anna. I was not feeling too well, so I decided on giving the sea a miss. Thanks to my Aunt Demi, not only was I an emotional wreck, it was also that time of the month. My kind and gentle cousin Kiri, who I loved very much was most concerned and every now and again kept coming over to see if I was okay. '*Of course I was okay,*' I constantly reassured him but that didn't stop him checking on me again and again. So I sat by myself on the warm pebbly shore trying to make the most of this hot, sticky day by reading a romantic novel that had come highly recommended to me by Irini. Just then, I was unexpectedly made aware of a pair of feet standing in front of me and whoever it was, was now shading me from my Cyprus sun. I stopped reading, closed my book and was ready to confront them and that's when I looked up and saw this gorgeous being standing over me - he looked as though he'd just stepped out from the waters where Aphrodite herself once bathed and had been sprinkled with her magic dust and beauty. The look on my face must have said it all. He was perfection.....sheer perfection!

'Hello cousin,' he said. 'Can I sit down and join you?'

'CAN YOU SIT DOWN AND JOIN ME?... INDEED YOU MAY!' I wanted to scream at the top of my voice but instead I just about said, 'Oh, yes of course.'

'Andreas,' he held out his hand. 'Your cousin Andreas.'

Summer, August 1977 Cyprus.

'Hello,' I frowned. 'You're my cousin?'

'And you are Sofia? Yes?' He spoke over me ignoring my question.

'Yes…yes I am. But how do you know my name?'

'I have been told that your mama is my mama's cousin.'

'So that makes us cousins too?'

'Yes…but third.'

'Oh, is that right?' I said, not taking in straight away what he was suggesting.

At that stage, I should have remembered third cousins were able to marry and that's what I guess he was implying.

'Have I interrupted you from your reading?'

'NO WAY!… ARE YOU MAD?… OF COURSE NOT!' I thought.

'No, no of course you haven't,' I said calmly.

'Good. May I sit down then?' He asked again

I nodded.

He started telling me how he wanted to become an airline pilot, *'to fulfil his childhood dream,'* and even though his lips were moving, I wasn't listening. It was as if there was nothing coming out. I just sat staring into his eyes, hypnotised and totally mesmerized by his divine presence.

'So who are you again?' I asked as he fell silent.

'I am your cousin Andreas,' he gave me a warm smile with a shake of his head, 'we have never met.'

No we hadn't because if we had I wouldn't have forgotten that face, those curly dark locks and gorgeous blue eyes. But why was he talking to me? Why wasn't he speaking to the other beauties on the beach? Was he mad?

'How long will you be in Cyprus for?' He asked.

'Um…two more weeks, just two I'm afraid.' And I remember thinking I wish it was more.

'Only two weeks? That is a shame.'

'Yes. It's my papa's belated fortieth birthday treat you see.'

'So how belated is it?'

'Only three years,' I sniggered and with that, we erupted into fits of laughter.

'Well it was lovely to eventually meet you Sofia,' he said, standing up to leave catching sight of his brother Manoli waving at him. 'I will

Summer, August 1977 Cyprus.

leave you now to continue reading your book. I hope to see you soon Sofia. Goodbye - *yasou.*'

'Okay. *Yasou*,' I replied.

I remember watching as he walked away from me, leaving me to continue reading my romantic novel. So I picked up my book and turned to the page I was reading before I'd been 'rudely' interrupted by the gorgeous Andreas....I wondered then if I'd ever see him again.

Day after day we visited the beach where I hoped I'd bump into him once again but it wasn't to be, he hadn't showed. Two whole weeks had passed without a single meeting so why had he arrived at the party? The Saturday before we were due to leave Cyprus for England, why now? I tried not to let his presence bother me, hoping he would perhaps even ignore me, but he didn't, which confused me even more, I would much rather he'd ignored me so that I could go back to England with a clear conscience, back to Jonathan whom I adored.

'Hello Sofia,' he smiled.

'Hello.'

'How are you? And how was your holiday?'

'I've been okay and my holiday was fab thanks,' I lied.

'What is fab? What do you mean Sofia?'

'Fab!...I mean really great! Except for earlier this morning when my auntie...'

I didn't want to really say anymore about what had happened.

'Why what happened, Sofia?' He asked.

'My Auntie Freda, she killed some chickens to cook for tonight's party,' I replied. 'Oh I see. You have never seen chickens being killed before?'

'No. It was so awful, she cut off their heads and they just ran around the yard until they died. My sisters and I couldn't stop screaming.'

'I am sorry. I am sure your auntie did not mean to upset you. I hear you are leaving on Monday.'

'Yes. Last day at the beach tomorrow,' I nodded, smiling back at him. 'I thought we may have bumped into each other before today,' I said.

I was about to tell Andreas how disappointed I was that we hadn't seen each other again, but instead, I stopped and turned my head to see what was causing such a noisy commotion and why everybody was cheering and whistling hysterically. That was when I caught sight of my papa in the middle of the dance floor. He'd suddenly turned into

Summer, August 1977 Cyprus.

Zorbra, jumping up in the air and throwing his arms around as he danced to his favourite Greek songs. My uncles were crouched down near him, clapping their hands encouraging him to dance some more, not that he needed encouragement. I'd seen this all before, papa dancing and throwing five pound notes in the air for the band not to stop and the more five pound notes he threw, the more the band played and the more the ouzo flowed the more papa danced.

'What were you saying, Sofia?!' Andreas shouted over the sound of music and noise.

I turned away from papa to look at Andreas and changed my mind. I changed my mind because he was my cousin and nothing could or should come of it. I would be going home after tomorrow and that would be that. No confusions, no mixed messages, just home.

'Nothing Andreas, nothing,' I replied.

Autumn, September 1977, England.

Chapter Eight

Our first day back at school had been a relief. I didn't normally like going, but I was glad to be back. Even the sight of Mrs Hodges, our music teacher, didn't upset me anymore. In the past I would have been be wary of her, she wasn't the most compassionate of teachers, having left a mark on me many years ago after having had an accident in one of her music lessons.

I still remember that day as if it had happened only yesterday - Wednesday, meat pie, mash and gravy day, followed by apple pie and custard. We'd just returned from the dining hall for one of our music lessons when, as soon as I sat down to sing, I needed to go to the toilet, but Mrs Hodges was so busy playing her piano she hadn't heard me calling - so inevitably - it happened.

After calling her about ten times or more, I stood up and began running around the classroom trying to hold on, and when I couldn't run anymore, I just stopped in the middle, started to cry and let it go. When she realized what I'd done, she stopped playing and ran out of the room to get Matron.

'I should have listened to her.'

I heard her telling Matron on her return.

'What happened, me dear?' Asked Matron.

I couldn't speak; I just cried, and I wanted to go home.

'Come on me dear,' she said, taking hold of my hand as she led me to her room. 'Let's get these wet clothes off.'

When Matron finished helping me dry myself she gave me an enormous pair of blue knickers and some dry socks, and placed my wet ones in a bag for me to take home. When Mrs Fairchild found out she came to see what had happened, but instead of being sympathetic, she decided to punish me by not allowing me to play with my friends at playtime. I was to stand by the old oak tree in the tiny playground, wearing the enormous blue knickers that hang half way down my legs.

Autumn, September 1977, England.

I still found that incident very upsetting, even after eleven years. But I never told papa about that day - I was good at keeping things to myself - I pretended it didn't bother me, pretended it hadn't happened. Just as I'd pretended I hadn't seen papa with Aunt Demi in the summerhouse almost a year ago.

Sometimes I wished I was still the only person who knew, because these days all mama and papa did was row, and who could blame mama; she'd been the perfect wife to him for seventeen years, and even though no one blamed her for the way she'd become - I found it hard listening to them rowing everyday.

Poor Lynsey and Mr and Mrs Bradshaw didn't quite know how to deal with it all, so they just went about minding their own business as they tried to continue with their daily routine, but it was very difficult for us all. These days I spent most of my free time at *yia'ya's*. Mr Bradshaw would take me as soon as I was ready and I normally got ready really quickly. I didn't want to leave mama but I also couldn't stay listening to them. Day in, day out, I just left them arguing.

'So, Harry!' She screamed. 'When did you throw our marriage in the toilet?!'

'Please calm down Elena, it wasn't like that.'

'So please tell me Harry. What was it like? When did it start, this filthy affair?!' He was standing by the fireplace in the sitting room, leaning on the mantelpiece looking down and he had a sudden flash back of the night it all began. He could see himself looking down at Demi; he raised her up into his arms as he made his way to the summerhouse.

'Tell me Harry...you owe me that!' She shouted, shaking him back from his thoughts.

'The night you were in hospital with Elizabeth,' he replied in a blank tone, still glaring downwards.

'Was that the day?! The day I had your daughter?! Please don't tell me that was the day!' She sobbed breaking down into tears.

'Yes,' he said, so ashamed he couldn't even look at her.

'I've been your wife for seventeen years, given you four beautiful daughters. And this is how you repay me?'

He turned his head to look at her and that look said it all, and Elena realized straight away what he was about to say.

'Oh... my...God, so you had an affair because I hadn't given you a son? A son to carry on the precious Constantine name?!' She screeched.

And hardly able to speak, he walked over to the drinks cabinet and poured himself a stiff glass of brandy. She knew him so well he thought - too well!

'I told you a long time ago,' she continued, 'even before we got married, that I would only stop loving you, when you stopped loving me. That is how much I loved you, Harry,' she said, calmly and in control. She stood up and walked straight out of the room.

'I never stopped loving you Elena....NEVER!' He exclaimed.

With that, she stopped, turned around and slowly walked back towards him, standing no more than an inch away from him, staring into his eyes, those now sombre blue eyes. She was looking at the man she once thought of as her prince - the love of her life, but she felt nothing for him now that was anything close to love, only pity. And with a frozen blank stare that didn't have an ounce of emotion, she stood for a moment allowing him to look at what he had done to her and what he was about to lose.

*　　*　　*　　*　　*　　*　　*　　*　　*

As the summer slowly turned her back on me, the cold winter soon returned and everything beautiful that had grown was gradually dying. I watched as the frost took over from the warm, sweet smelling days, taking away the wonderful sea of colour that had once dominated *yia'ya's* beautiful garden. Her home was my haven, a place that had the ability of making me feel safe, giving me a sense of peace for my mind and soul, protecting me from my fears, and giving me shelter from the outside world. She had become my rock.

Yia'ya tucked me into bed, and then brought up a tray with a large bowl of *av'go lemono* soup, a round of burnt, thickly buttered toast and a small dish with some warmed olive oil and cotton wool. I'd been feeling quite run down since we'd returned from Cyprus and the sudden change of climate resulted in me coming down with a very bad cold and an unbearable earache. It was amazing how *yia'ya* always seemed to have an answer to all our illnesses.

Autumn, September 1977, England.

I watched as she patiently dipped the cotton wool into the warmed olive oil.

'This should do it,' she said, gently placing the oil soaked cotton wool into my ears. 'You'll be as right as rain in the morning. I'll go and see who is knocking at the door. Now you get some rest and make sure you eat all your soup.'

'*Av'go lemono* soup, Greek medicine,' I said to myself. I looked over at the black and white photo of my *yia'ya* and *bapou* and smiled, and then taking my first delicious spoonful, I closed my eyes, letting the creamy-yellow rice melt slowly in my mouth, giving way for the lemony liquid to sooth my throat and bring back my taste buds. I pulled my toast apart, dunking it in like a spoon as I scooped up its yummy juices, but May had swung open my door with such a force that I almost jumped out of my skin and my soup out of its bowl. From the expression on my face, she realised what she'd done and she routinely put on one of her sorry faces running to embrace me.

'May! What are you doing here?!' I screamed a joyous scream. I was so delighted to see her. My dear and best friend May, with her friendly, happy face.

'I phoned your house but your mama told me you were here. Why didn't you say you were coming to your *yia'ya's?*'

'I'm not feeling too well, it was an unexpected visit.'

'What's that?' She asked, examining my ears.

'Cotton wool soaked in olive oil. Want to try some?'

'Oh God, no!' She scrunched her nose up. 'What's it for?'

'It's my *yia'ya's* cure for earache.' I could see she found it funny. 'Don't make fun.' Though it was too late we'd began to laugh.

'Well come on,' she said, taking a bite of my toast. 'Tell me about Cyprus then.'

'Why have you not been at school, Missy?' I asked.

'Believe it or not I had an earache too. Wish I'd known about your *yia'ya's* remedy,' she laughed. 'No seriously - the pain was killing me. Well, come on, I want to know everything.'

'There's not much to say really,' I said, not looking up at her as I continued eating.

'So why don't I believe you?'

'Really, I'm telling you the truth,' I said. 'Would you like some soup?'

Autumn, September 1977, England.

'Yes May,' said *yia'ya*, as she re-entered my room to check if I'd finished.

'Would you like some?'

'No thank you *yia'ya*. I'm not hungry. I'll just put on my pyjamas and get ready for bed.'

Yia'ya took the tray, kissed us goodnight and left.

I laid down, pushing back the covers ready for May to climb in. We always slept together in the double bed, talking for hours and only falling asleep when the sun came up and the birds began to sing. In no time at all she'd put on her pyjamas and was next to me in bed, waiting to hear about my holiday in Cyprus, her head in her hand using her elbow as support on a propped up pillow.

'Well,' she said.

'Well, it was very hot.'

'And?'

'And when we arrived, my uncles were all there to meet us. It must have been the hottest summer on record. It was unbearable.'

'Unbearable?' She shrugged, with suspicion in her voice.

'Yes, unbearable,' I replied, tempting her away from this conversation.

'You haven't been back to Cyprus for four years and all you can say is, 'it was hot and unbearable.' Where's all the enthusiasm you had before you got there? Sofia what's wrong?'

I laid in total silence, just staring up at the ceiling. I knew this day would come, I just didn't know it would be now.

'Sofia? Now you're scaring me. Say something Sofia.'

'It's okay, really it is, there's nothing wrong.'

'No it's not okay. You know I can sense your feelings Sofia. Tell me what's wrong.'

'Sunday, the day before we left, Aunt Demi lost her baby,' I said calmly, not looking at May, not taking my stare away from the ceiling.

There was a silence that felt so long and so still. I was hoping May would say something - anything.

'But...your Aunt Demi can't have children?' She replied thoughtfully.

'No, it seems that's not all together true. It turns out it's my Uncle Mike who can't have children.'

'What! Your Aunt Demi was pregnant and your Uncle can't have

81

children? Whose was it then? What happened? How did you find out? Sofia?!' She shrieked, not able to get it out quick enough.

'She fell into the sea, out of the speed boat. My Uncle Mike had had far too much to drink; he was going too fast and lost control… She fell out and lost her baby,' I said, tears were now streaming down my face.

'But….who's baby was it if not your Uncle Mikes? Do you know Sofia?'

I didn't want to say because I didn't want anyone to know but I also couldn't keep it to myself anymore.

'I think it must have been papa's baby,' I said, slowly turning to face her.

May sat up hardly believing what she'd just heard me say. 'Sofia you're messing about, right?'

'I wish I was May. I wish I was.' Now I was sobbing, sobbing with all my heart.

'But what about your mama? What about your mama, Sofia? Does she know?'

'Yes she does now. That's why I'm here. I don't think I can bear to listen to them rowing anymore.'

'What about Christina and Irini?'

'They know about the baby but I'm the only one who knew about papa and Aunt Demi.'

'You mean you knew and you didn't tell me? We tell each other everything!'

'I wanted to every time I saw you. Every time May, but I was so frightened. I just tried to pretend it wasn't happening,' I wept.

'How long have you known?'

'Since last Christmas. I saw them together in the summerhouse.'

'Oh God. What's going to happen?' May whispered tearfully

'I'm not sure, May. It's the worst thing that's ever happen. I'm so, so scared.'

She lay down and embraced me, holding me while the tears streamed down our faces and our fears occupied our minds. Tonight we wouldn't be laughing and talking 'til dawn, nor would we be awake to welcome the birds as they began to sing.

As the darkness hung all around, it slowly calmed us down and we

Autumn, September 1977, England.

eventually fell asleep in each other's arms. Tonight.... there was nothing more to be said.

*   *   *   *   *   *   *   *   *

After the unforeseen event that happened on our last day in Cyprus, where everybody's lives had been turned up side down, my poor Uncle Mike couldn't come to terms with it all, and no amount of reasoning from my Uncles, Nick and George, could make it better. He felt humiliated, confused, disgusted, depressed - all of these rolled into one - he was suicidal!

The family were most concerned about his condition, keeping a constant watch over him, so much so, that he came to stay with us at Holly Blue after papa had moved out. Mama was brilliant, cooking and cleaning for him, taking him out with her on long walks in the cold forest, even encouraging him to go and talk with a psychologist. She made him her responsibility, throwing herself into overdrive.

The weekly visits to the psychologist had become quite therapeutic for both of them. She found speaking to a total stranger about what had troubled her for such a long time a relief, and even though my uncle was suffering terribly, mama had been suffering in silence for much longer and that's why she found it easy to take charge. I suppose deep down she was half expecting this to come to a head.

Unfortunately, Uncle Mike's condition took a turn for the worse. His despair turned into fear and he slowly found leaving the house a struggle. He was terrified, terrified of the thoughts that were trying to escape from the depths of his mind - black and charcoal-grey were the only colours he could see now. And there was a voice in his head - his voice - torturing him with ideas that were so dreadful and shocking that his weak mind couldn't fight anymore. A voice telling him his life was meaningless, worthless, and hopeless. He couldn't see the light at the end of the tunnel; he stopped searching because there wasn't one for him. Demi had seen to that a long time ago.

Sadly, my Uncle Mike's funeral was to become the second in the family that I would be attending, and even though I was a lot older since *bapou* Christos had died, it was not to be any easier.

The day of the funeral was cold, dull and grey, reflecting my

Autumn, September 1977, England.

emotions, and the rain was coming down hard and sharp with no intention of stopping. I put on my black dress, a pair of woollen tights and boots, and as I stood looking at my reflection in the long mirror in my bedroom, there was a knock at my door and my cousin Helen poked her head around it, giving me a sad smile. It took me back to last Christmas when she had found me here panicking because I wasn't ready. Who would have thought that not quite a year later the reflection staring back at me would be of me dressed in black attending my uncle's funeral?

'Come in, Helen.'

'Oh! Sofia,' she said, running into my arms.

'Are you alright?'

'Yes,' she nodded. 'How are you?'

'Do you remember the last time we were here in my room?'

'Yes.'

'Who would have thought, eh?'

'Who would?' She shook her head, looking down at the floor.

'Is everybody downstairs?'

'Yes. Poor *yia'ya's* lying down on the sofa in the sitting room.'

'I'm not sure she'll get over this one. Let's go down, shall we?' I said sympathetically, taking hold of her hand.

I closed my bedroom door behind me walking slowly along the corridor and just before we went down we stopped at the exact spot where Jonathan had stood on my birthday, when he had called me up to join him. We watched from the banister as our family and friends gathered in small groups in the hall, chatting quietly amongst themselves waiting for the funeral procession to arrive.

I squeezed Helen's hand, a gesture that said it was time for us to go down and face whatever this horrid day had in store. We went outside and waited for the hearse to stop, gradually coming in to view as it slowly pulled up in front of our house. That was the moment it hit me, until then I hadn't believed it to be true but now as it came to a halt, I tightened my lips trying to fight back the tears. We bowed our heads in a mark of respect, and I felt the knot in my stomach tighten as the funeral directors got out placing all the beautiful wreaths and flowers on the roofs of the waiting limousines. Then, I took hold of Christina and

Autumn, September 1977, England.

Irini's hand and led them to our car where Mr Bradshaw was standing with the door wide open. He helped us get in and we were off. No one had anything to say, not even little Anna, who was now sitting in a sombre way and Kiri just looked down at his feet, tears rolling down from his cheeks and onto his jacket, every now and again he'd pull out a hanky and blow his nose. I just stared out of the window, frightened by the sound that was coming from the pounding rain as it struck down hard upon the car, thumping and hammering as if trying to get in.

The head funeral director walked in front of the moving hearse as he guided it down Holly Blue Lane to the main road and as we turned the corner I watched as our uncle began his last journey.

When St Mary's Church came into view, I knew she'd be saluting him and receiving us with open arms as she had done so many times before, but today's visit was to be one of the most difficult yet, because the taking of ones own life would be hard for everyone to understand, and hard to accept.

It looked as though the rain wouldn't give way, but as the hearse came to a stop outside the church, it did just that. My uncles helped carry the coffin into the church for the burial service and sat it in the centre of the nave facing the altar. The coffin was then opened and an Icon of Christ was placed in Uncle Mike's hands. A wreath had been placed on his forehead and a hand cross near his head.

My cousins Fivo, Christos and Kiri handed out candles to the mourners who, on receiving the light from the priest, held them lit throughout the service until near the end. After the priest's dismissal, our friends joined us as we said our last goodbye, kissing either the hand cross, which was set on the side of the coffin or the Icon in my uncles hands. The coffin was then closed and carried out to the hearse as the choir boys and girls sang, whilst the church bells rung slowly. The funeral cortege proceeded to the cemetery where a short graveside service was sung by the priest, and only when the coffin had been lowered into the ground did the sun come out.

The hard truth was, yes, my Uncle Mike had taken his own life and he was gone, that was the reality of it. We would have to live with what he'd done and live with wondering if we'd all done enough and why we hadn't been able to reach him.

My first summer in Jersey, 1978.

Chapter Nine

The weeks turned into months and the cold dark winter gently thawed away and disappeared. Life as we knew it could never be the same and Uncle Mike would never be forgotten. We'd heard Aunt Demi had gone to stay with some relatives in America, never to be seen, or heard of, again. And as for my papa, he now lived alone in his London apartment.

Mama forbade him from coming anywhere near the house, so the only time we saw him was when she was having a good day and would allow us to visit him; asking Mr Bradshaw to take and collect us. Even though mama tried getting on with her life, it still felt strange seeing her without papa by her side; they had, over the years, almost become one person. I used to think mama was so delicate, a woman that relied on him for everything, but it's amazing how we find an inner strength when we search for it and mama had finally found hers. So, as the winter turned into spring, then summer once more, I visited my friends at *yia'ya's*, as I also, tried to get on with my life. We had of course grown up and left behind the games we used to play.

I'd turned sixteen last April and even though I would always be a big kid at heart, some things would have to be kept as fond memories. We were off from school for seven whole weeks in the summer and this year mama agreed to let me visit Aunt Margaret's sister Violet who lived by the sea in Jersey. It took quite a bit of convincing from Aunt Margaret but she eventually came round to the idea and thought it may actually do me some good.

I would be going to the coast to spend two weeks by the sea - two wonderful weeks!

We set off early in order to avoid the traffic and I was so excited because I'd never been away with anyone but my family before, and if papa had been around he probably wouldn't have allowed it, but he wasn't around and I was going; going to the sea with Uncle Henry,

My first summer in Jersey, 1978.

Aunt Margaret, Grandma Guilbey and Sarah. The only person missing was Jonathan, though that couldn't be helped, now that he lived in London near the university where he was studying law, and unfortunately couldn't just drop everything and join us. Yet I had every intention in making the most of this trip because I loved being by the sea and even though it wasn't going to be anything like Cyprus, that didn't mean it wouldn't be fun. I made sure to pack my canvas and oils because Auntie Violet's house, I was told, was right on the seafront with spectacular views. I couldn't wait! It normally took about an hour to get to the airport and a half hour flight to Jersey, but Uncle Henry had implied that we would be stopping for a break, so our journey would take slightly longer. We actually stopped by a lay-by park so we could have some tea. English tea and sandwiches, it was all so very grand.

'Have another, lovey,' said Aunt Margaret, as she shoved another tray of watercress sandwiches under my nose.

'Thanks auntie, but I've had enough.'

'Would you like a sausage roll instead, lovey?'

'No thank you, I've had plenty.'

'Oh, you young girls,' said Grandma Guilbey, as she slurped down her tea, 'are always watching your figures. When we were young there was none of all that.'

Grandma Guilbey always slurped her tea. I think that was because she had false teeth - false teeth, whiskers and plump reddish-pink cheeks.

'Yes grandma, we know how you all went without during the war,' said Sarah, quickly coming to my rescue.

'Well we did,' she said, slurping some more of her tea. 'I'll have another sausage roll.' She rattled.

I turned to look at Sarah and we began to laugh, Uncle Henry joined in then Aunt Margaret too. Grandma Guilbey just carried on eating, eating her sausage roll and slurping her tea, and we just laughed and laughed!

'Come on mother,' said Uncle Henry to Aunt Margaret. 'Let's make a move.' Grandma Guilbey quickly polished off the rest of the food from her plate, brushed away the crumbs from her lap and was ready to go.

When we eventually got to the airport, Sarah and I were so thrilled

My first summer in Jersey, 1978.

to be going on a plane together. Uncle Henry agreed to let us sit by ourselves a few rows in front. We clicked our safety belts simultaneously and listened with anticipation as the air hostess ran us through the safety checks, and before we could say Jiminy Cricket, the plane was speeding down the run-way. We were served a glass of fresh orange juice, yet as soon as we'd drank it we'd landed. That's how quick the flight was!

Sarah and I sat, squashed, in the back of the car with Grandma Guilbey as Uncle Henry drove us along the seafront with Aunt Margaret playing navigator. Straight away I could see myself sitting with my face buried into Christina thinking I was going to die on the mountains in Cyprus, and I closed my eyes, automatically feeling the cool sea breeze blowing all around me, messing my hair and awakening my senses 'til my lungs were full and I could smell that distinctiveness of the British coast - salty, slimy seaweed, mixed with fried sugared doughnuts. As the smell of the sugared doughnuts got my tummy rumbling, forcing me to open my eyes, I caught sight of the famous Queen Elizabeth castle in the distance where the vastness of the sea made it look almost like a miniature model, as if it were so small I could pick it up with one hand.

When we came to the end of the road that ran along the coast, we turned into a narrow street where the houses were all joined together. It may have been the longest street in the whole world, even longer than my *yia'ya* Athena's, there were terraced houses, rows and rows of them all looking the same, all identical. Finally, when we'd got to the end of *the longest street in the world*, we made a sharp turn and started making our way up a steep hill that eventually led us to Auntie Violet's house.

'*We're here!*' Uncle Henry sang, honking the car horn as he came to a sudden stop.

As Auntie Violet ran out from this amazing white house with blue shutters and a blue front door Uncle Henry began unloading the boot and Aunt Margaret got out of the car, but there were no big scenes and tears liked the ones in Cyprus with Auntie Freda - this was all very civilized. Sarah and I helped grandma out of the car; the long drive had left her a little stiff due to the arthritis in her knees.

My first summer in Jersey, 1978.

'Come in grandma, come in. I've made a fresh pot of tea,' Auntie Violet said, leading her into the house.

The smell of boiling cabbage was the first thing to hit me. From the very moment I stepped into the hall, from the first intake of breath, that's what I could smell, just like school dinners, cabbage and apple pie - I loved apple pie.

Apple pie and custard! YUMMY!

'I hope you like cabbage,' laughed Auntie Violet, looking behind her as she led us into the sitting room.

'Vi,' said Aunt Margaret, taking hold of my hand to introduce me. 'This is Sofia.'

'Hello Auntie Violet,' I smiled.

'Hello Sofia. You're so much more beautiful than I was told,' she smiled, glancing over at Aunt Margaret. 'Call me Aunt Vi lovey, everybody does, and don't believe what my sister may have told you, I'm not like your Aunt Margi, I'm the sensible one; never got married. Take it from me, give away your heart lovey and sure as pie - it will be broken.' 'Oh, sorry,' I sympathized.

'Don't be lovey, not your fault. Anyway I'd much rather live here with Mittens these days.'

'Is that Mittens sitting on the windowsill?'

'Yes. That's my lazy girl.'

'Did you call her that because of her little white paws?'

'Yes lovey and she'll have you stroking her 'til the cows come home if you let her.'

'She must love staring out at the sea. I bet she sits there for hours.'

'All day long, eats and sleeps, that's all she does, no good for catching mice though - far too strenuous,' she chuckled. 'I must check on the pie lovey.'

'I'll help you,' smiled Aunt Margaret.

'Why not show Sofia your room, Sarah?' Uncle Henry suggested, taking a look out of the window where Mittens was laying. 'Isn't this lovely?' He said, his gaze taking in the view.

The upstairs of Aunt Vi's house was as I contemplated, just like the downstairs - floral prints everywhere. Floral carpet, floral curtains, even the walls were decorated with floral wallpaper. The bedroom

My first summer in Jersey, 1978.

where Sarah and I were to be sleeping faced the sea and it was absolutely breathtaking. I could see the Queen Elizabeth castle in the far distance and a million tiny sailing boats by the seas-edge swaying from side to side as they sat without their captains, ready and waiting for tomorrow to arrive so they could sail onto another great adventure.

I began taking out my canvas and oils hoping I could paint another masterpiece. It wasn't everyday I had such an amazing view from my bedroom window, and painting it meant engraving it in my mind to keep forever. I would take it back home with me to share with Christina and Irini.

'I hope you don't mind Sarah? I'll come down later,' I asked, sticking my nose in my paint box.

'No, that's okay. Mum will call you when supper's on the table.'

'Thanks,' I said, not looking up as I searched for my favourite brushes.

'Okay, happy painting,' she smiled, closing the bedroom door behind her.

This was wonderful, just what the doctor would have ordered. I was once again at peace with the world and at one with Mother Nature. My trusted canvas and oils took me to far and away places, places I could only dream of and places I wanted to stay forever. After what seemed like only a few minutes, I heard Aunt Margaret calling me to come down.

'Sofia! Sofia lovey! Supper is ready and there's someone here who wants to say hello!'

'I won't be a mo auntie!' I called back.

'Okay lovey!'

I dipped my brushes into a jar filled with turps and hurriedly made my way downstairs to the dining room. To my surprise I found Jonathan standing there.

'Jonathan!' I screamed aloud.

'Hello Sofia!' He said scooping me up into his arms. 'Surprised?'

'What are you doing here?' I asked, my face lit up, I was so thrilled and suddenly becoming aware of everyone staring at me - I blushed!

'I convinced my lecturer to let me fly out to the sea for some very important research.'

'That's great, how long are you here for?'

'Well, I have a lot of research to do,' he smirked. 'So I'll need at least

90

My first summer in Jersey, 1978.

two weeks.'

'Come on loveys, lets have supper,' said Aunt Vi, taking hold of our arms.

The smile on my face must have said it all; I was in heaven, in sheer and utter bliss. My stomach was full with so many butterflies I could hardly eat, they were dancing with such excitement, leaving me feeling dizzy to the point where it had become impossible and I couldn't eat any more, not even my favourite apple pie and custard. I put down my spoon and asked if I could leave the table.

'Are you finished lovey?' Aunt Vi frowned. 'Didn't you like the pie?'

'Oh, no!' I heartedly replied. 'It was lovely thanks but I just can't eat anymore.'

'I'm also finished Aunt Vi,' Jonathan said, putting down his spoon smiling towards me, 'would you like to go for a walk Sofia?'

'Yes okay.'

'I'm finished as well mum,' said Sarah, shovelling the last spoonful of apple pie into her mouth. 'Can I go for a walk?'

Aunt Margaret looked at Jonathan, then at Uncle Henry but before she could answer, Uncle Henry patted his knee and said, 'come and sit with your old dad Sarah.' In a flash and without a second thought she was up and in his arms. I suddenly remembered all the nights papa would come home after a hard day's work at his office, that's all he wanted was for me to sit with him. I missed that very much.

'If you go for a walk with Sofia and Jonathan, then who will I play Scrabble with? You know grandma cheats,' Uncle Henry whispered.

'Yes bless her,' she giggled in his ear, 'she can't spell either.'

'Well do you want to play?'

'Yes, I'll run upstairs and fetch it,' she kissed him on the forehead, and turning to Jonathan said, 'sorry I'll have to come for a walk with you another day,' then she fled upstairs to find the Scrabble.

'Thanks dad,' acknowledged Jonathan, 'ready?' He said to me.

'Yes, I'll get my jacket,' I nodded.

The back of Aunt Vi's garden led directly to the beach. Jonathan took hold of my hand. 'You okay Sofia?' He asked.

'*No, I'm not okay, I've missed you so much*' – Is what I really wanted to say but I was nervous about letting him know how I felt so instead I lied, 'yes, I've been okay.' 'I've missed you Sofia.'

My first summer in Jersey, 1978.

'How's university?' Gulping back a scream I asked, paying no attention to what he'd just said.

'Fantastic! It's so huge and the students come from all over the world. The lectures are interesting but so intense.'

He was speaking with such enthusiasm in his voice, I was jealous that he could find something else so exciting, something other than his life at home in Epping where we lived. I suppose I didn't want to share him with anything or anyone and I was feeling a little insecure. Maybe, under the circumstances with what had happened with my papa it was a normal reaction.

'Don't sound too enthusiastic I may want to join you.'

'Oh Sofia, you'd love it.' He stopped to look at me. 'You're trembling. Are you cold? Here have my jacket,' he said, taking it off and wrapping it around my shoulders.

'Thanks,' I said, looking up into his beautiful blue eyes. 'Well, tell me more.'

'There's a theatre, its own chapel and a library like you wouldn't believe, not like the tiny one at Wilbury Manor. It's enormous!' He excelled flinging his arms out.

'Perfect for the *perfect* scholar then, not like me. I'm hardly academic.'

'Who cares about academics? I've never seen anyone paint like you. Your paintings are incredible.'

'Are they? Do you really think so?' I shrugged, 'you're just saying that.'

'No they are. They're as fantastic and as fabulous as you. When I look at them it's as if I can read your every thought.'

'Wow! I didn't realise you looked into my paintings and my mind.'

'Always and every time I look at one,' he spoke sincerely.

'I'd best stop painting then,' I said, playfully teasing him with a nudge.

'Why, what are you scared I'll see?'

'I'm not scared you'll see anything.'

'Not anything?'

'No.'

All of a sudden there was a huge bang coming from the sky, followed by another bang and another, then a spectacular spray of colour.

'Quick! Sofia run! Run!' He called, pulling me towards the massive crowd of people who'd gathered on the beach watching the fireworks

My first summer in Jersey, 1978.

display coming from the castle. 'It's the finale!'

We ran as fast as we could, edging through the crowd as we made our way near the front. Then hand in hand, we watched and listened as the music and the fireworks were working together, swoosh bang, swoosh bang! Bang! Bang! They exploded in the air performing an intimate synchronization, becoming one as they entertained us, wooing us and making us roar and cheer with excitement. They were powerful together and at the same time so gentle. It was exactly the same feeling Jonathan and I had as we stood in the middle of a thousand others. Although in our hearts there was nobody else around, just him and me. Wrapped in his jacket and in his arms, we were alone, nobody else mattered and nobody else existed.

I could feel the warmth of his body next to mine, our faces so close that I melted into the sweetness of his embrace.

'Well, what am I thinking now Mr Academic?' I whispered to him.

He didn't answer, he didn't have to, instead he just tenderly kissed me.

*   *   *   *   *   *   *   *   *

'Sofia wake up!' Sarah called. 'It's such a lovely day. Mum and dad are taking us out.'

'What time is it?' I groaned, my eyes shut with the covers pulled up over my head.

'Nine o'clock and we're going to be late if we don't get up now!'

'Where are we going?'

'Just out for the day, come on.'

'Do you think Aunt Margaret would let me give it a miss today? I'm tired.'

'Not surprisingly. What time did you and my brother return home last night?'

'Not late. We stayed and watched the fireworks display.'

'Was it fun?'

'Yes, it was,' I mumbled peering out from under the blanket.

'You like Jonathan, don't you Sofia?' She said raising an eyebrow.

'Yes, we're good friends,' I answered sheepishly; I could feel myself beginning to blush - again.

'No, I mean you *really* like him, don't you?' She asked again, this

93

time with an inquisitive tone - one that said she knew.

'Hey Missy, what are you getting at?' I said, chucking back my covers. 'Come here!'

'No! No!' She screamed.

'Oh yes! Yes!' I said, pinning her down on the bed.

'No Sofia, don't tickle me. Don't!'

'Who do I like?' I said, tickling her 'til she surrendered. 'Who Miss Nosey Parker?

'Jonathan! You like Jonathan!' Screaming some more, she kicked her legs down on the mattress.

'Who do I like?' I laughed.

There was a knock at the door but with the racket that was going on we didn't notice Aunt Margaret come into the room.

'Girls, girls come on. Why are you not ready?'

'Because I'm tickling Sarah to death Aunt Margaret,' I said out of breath and exhausted.

'Girls! We'll be late if you don't hurry.'

'Do I have to come along auntie?' I asked.

'Are you not well lovey?'

'No, I mean yes I am well. It's just that I'd like to do some more work on my painting if it's okay with you?' I said, letting Sarah go.

'Oh it's lovely, Sofia,' she said proudly looking over at my canvas. 'Well of course, if that's what you want do.'

'Is Jonathan coming with us mum?' Sarah inquired looking over at me and giving me a playful smile. Her question having a deeper motive.

'No, he also has some work to do. Now come on Sarah lovey, you must get ready.'

Aunt Margaret looked at me and smiled, she knew why I wanted to stay, she had also been young and in love once. I tried hard to hide it from her but you couldn't hide anything from Aunt Margaret and even though she knew why I wanted to stay, she approved. If it had been anyone else but Jonathan I think she would have kicked up a fuss, but it wasn't, it was Jonathan, her son - her pride - and she trusted he would take care of me.

I heard the car drive off and I ran to the window to wave them goodbye and Uncle Henry honked the car horn, he enjoyed doing that. I didn't know where Jonathan was so I went into the kitchen to

My first summer in Jersey, 1978.

make myself some tea.

'Would you like a cuppa?' He said, holding up the kettle. 'I think it's from the Iron Age.'

'Wow! You frightened me!' I screeched, holding my stomach for dear life. 'Do you think it works?' I joked.

'Let's find out shall we. Now you sit yourself down, I've got it all under control.' I did as I was told so as not to disappoint him. I sat and watched as he tried to find his way around this multi-coloured kitchen. Its' Orange, green and browns made it looked as though we were in some kind of psychedelic disco straight out of the sixties.

He was hilarious, sticking his head into cabinets as their doors flew apart, opening draws and slamming them shut, rattling whatever it was they were filled with. He looked absolutely charming as he frantically prepared to impress me with his culinary skills, so much so that it didn't mattered if he could cook or not, the sheer fact was, he was pure entertainment and *that* was sufficient.

'D'you like eggs?' He asked, rattling an egg box in one hand and a frying pan in the other.

I nodded an amused, 'yes.'

'Good, because they're one of the only things I can cook. Your breakfast won't be long, me lady,' he said, taking a bow.

'Take your time, dear sir. I'm finding all this quite entertaining.'

'You're finding this entertaining me lady?' He smirked and offered his hand.

'Yes, quite amusing dear sir.'

'Can me lady hear music?'

'Yes,' I replied, trying to keep a straight face. 'Can you dear sir?'

'Yes. Your voice is sweet music to my ears. Would you care for this dance?'

'I would indeed,' I said, joining him on the 'dance floor.' As he pulled me closer to him, we danced round and around this *teensy weensy* little kitchen as if we were Lord and Lady of the Manor. He led the way and I willingly followed.

'Now that you have me here alone dear sir, what will you do with me?' I asked, frivolously. My perfectly curled eyelashes flickered at him giving an impish look.

'I will kiss me lady's sweet lips, if she wishes me to.'

'She wishes that very much,' I replied, I was going to get what I so

My first summer in Jersey, 1978.

desperately longed for - his kiss.

'Sofia, I lo…'

'No, Jonathan. Don't,' I quickly interrupted him.

'Sofia?' he whispered with a shrug.

'Jonathan… Shh, don't say it.'

I put my hand on his mouth to stop him and he began to kiss it, his soft lips speaking to me without having to utter a word. They found their way from my hand up my arm to my shoulder. He was kissing my neck, kissing me as if he'd kissed me like this a million times before. I felt the goose bumps rise on my body and I was powerless, wanting to submit to him. I had feelings stirring inside of me I hadn't been aware of before and my heart was racing. I took hold of his hand and put it upon my chest so he could feel my heartbeat.

'Can you feel what you're doing to me?' I could hardly get the words out.

'No different to what you are doing to me,' he replied, his lips felt as though they'd permanently fixed themselves on me.

'Jonathan I've never done anything like this before,' I gasped. 'I'm sorry… I'm sorry, please stop, I can't do this. I've spoilt everything haven't I?'

'Sofia?'

'Yes, Jonathan.'

'Smile.'

'What?'

'Just, smile if you love me.'

'You're embarrassing me,' I coyly looked away from his stare, not giving too much away.

'I love you Sofia,' he said cautiously. He could see I was nervous. 'I've loved you from the very moment I first saw you.'

'Please, just hold me and don't say anymore.' So he held me in his arms, not making me feel as if I'd spoilt this special moment. My head was ruling my heart yet I knew how I felt about Jonathan, so it would only be a matter of time 'til that day would arrive and I would be ready to tell him I loved him, only then would I let my heart do as it desired. But today was not that day.

As the days and nights sped by we had become inseparable, sharing

96

My first summer in Jersey, 1978.

a closeness that I never thought possible of having with another person. This was different to the closeness I felt with my family and my friends, not even the same as what I had with my sisters and best friend May. I was in love, and the very thought of not being able to see Jonathan when the summer was over upset me beyond belief. We promised to write everyday and see each other whenever possible, whenever time would permit. But we were here together now and that's all that mattered. All I wanted was to spend every breathing moment with him. We had spent most of our evenings on the beach at the back of Aunt Vi's beautiful house. Every night Jonathan would bring a blanket for us to sit on and a flask of Uncle Henry's special coffee, two mugs and some doughnuts. Hour after hour would pass us by as we lay under the stars with the only sounds coming from the waves as they left ripples on the shore and of the crackling sticks as they burnt in the small fire he'd light to keep the cool sea breeze at bay.

But the days had sadly flown away very swiftly, flown away like swallows leaving behind them the end of the summer. We would soon be leaving this fantastic island, and sadly were now spending our last night here. Jonathan had promised me a surprise trip in the morning saying, *'dress warmly because we'll be out 'til late.'*

'Where are we going?' I asked eagerly.

'I've never met a more impatient girl than you Sofia.'

'I can't wait 'til the morning,' I pleaded, pathetically trying to put out the fire.

'You'll have to,' he said, stumping out the remains with his feet. 'Sofia stop, I'll do that. You're going to burn yourself,' he laughed.

But I wouldn't listen, 'no I won't stop!' I screamed. 'Not until you tell me,' I stropped, waving my arms in the air, jumping up and down on the smouldering ashes.

With that he grabbed hold of me, spinning me round until I fell into his arms. 'You've got sugar on your lips,' he said, trying to wipe it off with his hand.

But teasingly I moved my head from side to side.

'Okay, if that's what you want, I'll kiss it off then,' he laughed and then kissed me. 'You taste good,' he smirked, savouring the sugar from my mouth.

My first summer in Jersey, 1978.

We couldn't keep our hands off each other, not for a single moment. We shared every breath, every touch, however small. Every look we gave one another said how we felt. I didn't want to return to the house, not just yet, for I would have to leave him 'til the morning and that wouldn't do.

I didn't want to be without him, I would miss him too much.

By the time we returned home everyone had gone to bed, only Mittens came to the door to greet us. We said our goodnights and I quietly tiptoed up to my room where I found Sarah fast asleep and snoring. I gently kissed her forehead and got into my bed. I always kissed Christina and Irini when we slept together in the same room at *yia'ya's* house, but I didn't have Christina and Irini here with me now, I had Sarah instead.

I laid in the darkness just thinking of him. The past two weeks here with Jonathan were whirling around in my mind, occupying my thoughts 'til I couldn't keep my eyes open anymore, and as the night quickly turned into day, I fell asleep with the warm sun entering my room trying to wake me. I could hear the sound of the seagulls outside fishing for their early morning feast as they gracefully flew over the golden, translucent sea and I pulled the blanket over my head.

All too soon there was a gentle tap on my door and Aunt Margaret entered with a mug of tea, some toast and a message from Jonathan. She put the tray down on the little table by my bed and sat down next to me. I could feel her gentleness as she stroked my hair and for a moment I thought it was my mama.

'Jonathan's waiting for you downstairs lovey.'

'I know,' I nodded from beneath my blanket.

'He's sent you up some tea and toast, just the way you like it.'

'Burnt?' I sighed under my breath, managing a smile to myself.

'*Very!*'

'Mmm, smells lovely.'

'Well, I'll leave you to it. Don't let your tea get cold lovey.'

'I won't,' I shook my head. I wasn't ready to get up just yet, but as I pulled my blanket further over my head I knew I should because Jonathan was downstairs ready and waiting and the least I could do was not let the tea that he'd sent up get cold. So I slowly pushed away my blanket and forced myself to sit up.

98

My first summer in Jersey, 1978.

'Burnt toast,' I said, looking at the tray, and I felt a warm glow travel over my body. 'He remembered,' I sighed. I jumped out of bed and ran downstairs. 'Jonathan! Jonathan where are you?!' I called out to him.

'He's gone for a walk on the beach with Sarah,' said Aunt Vi, poking her head out from the kitchen. 'Would you like a cuppa lovey?'

'No thanks. I've got one already Aunt Vi.'

'He won't be long lovey. Sarah was feeling a bit, well, you know.'

'Left out?' I said, finishing what she was going to say. 'Okay, I'll go up and get ready.'

'Don't you worry yourself lovey she's fine. Just misses him. You know.'

'Yes.... I know.'

I walked up to my room wondering if Sarah begrudged me and Jonathan spending so much time together, leaving no room for anybody else, I hoped she didn't. I wasn't here to shut her out. She was his little sister and I suppose she felt as though she was loosing him, but she wasn't, Jonathan would always be her big brother and he would always love his sister, as I did mine.

By the time I got dressed they were back from their walk and as the back door swung open I could hear them giggling with each other. 'Jonathan! I'm ready!' I called out to him again, swiftly making my way back downstairs.

'Good morning, sleepy head,' he said, kissing me on the cheek.

'Good morning. How was your walk Sarah?' I asked her.

'It was great Sofia. You should've come,' she replied, putting her arms around Jonathan and giying him a loving squeeze.

'Next time ey?'

'Okay. Come here Mittens. Are you hungry?' She said, picking her up and heading to the kitchen.

'Thanks for the toast by the way.'

'You're welcome.'

'You remembered.'

'Burnt.'

'Yes.'

'Are you ready to go?'

'Yes, but where are we going?' I asked again.

'You'll see.'

The drive around this picturesque island looked almost unreal.

My first summer in Jersey, 1978.

Overflowing with history and charm, it was, unsurprisingly, the birth place of Lillie Langtry, the beauty who was mistress and friend to the Prince of Wales, the then Prince Edward. She was what romance stood for and for such a romantic as I it was the perfect place to be. Jonathan had shrugged off my passionate enthusiasm about Miss Langtry pretending to cringe in a most typically chauvinistic way. But I couldn't help but fall in love with it, with its castles and piers, its hilltops and golden beaches. This beautiful island was so full of culture and heritage.

'Jonathan, this is beautiful, the most beautiful place I have ever seen.'

'Mulberry Hill! The eighth Wonder of the World!' He cried.

He stopped the car for a moment allowing us to take in this 'Wonder' and then he looked at me with that loving look of his, the look I'd become quite accustomed to. I could see the pleasure in his eyes knowing he had pleased me, and as we drove up the steep hills and back down again I knew Jonathan was the one I would have wanted to share all of this with. It didn't take long to drive around the whole of the island but I would have been quite happy just seeing the same sights over and over again just as long as it was with him.

After he'd gone around, what felt like a hundred times, he found a secluded place and parked where nobody could disturb us.

'Come here Sofia,' he said, making room for me to sit next to him at the steering wheel. 'No Jonathan. No, I can't drive,' I said, my eyes widened with excitement.

'I dare you,' he said teasing mischievously.

'No.'

'I'll teach you then,' he grinned.

'Okay, it's your head,' I said. I grabbed hold of the wheel and we were off, Jonathan at the control pedals whilst I steered the car. I was like a maniac, driving all over the place, going into every ditch and hole, screaming with both thrill and fear.

'Go Sofia! Go!' He yelled.

'Jonathan!' I screamed, squinting my eyes as we were about to hit a large tree.

He quickly slammed down on the brakes. I threw back my head with relief and laughed, I laughed so much. 'Are we dead yet?'

I looked over at him, threw open the door and got out of the car. My heart was still racing as I began to run, my stride now going just as

My first summer in Jersey, 1978.

fast as I waved my arms through the virtual crowd. Yet there wasn't a single soul to be seen, just green hills, the golden sea and blue sky. I closed my eyes wanting to capture this moment forever like a photograph, wanting to keep it with me always, and when I stopped running, I could still feel the cool wind as it moved over my body, in my hair and on my face and that's when I felt him put his arms around me.

'I've got something for you,' he said, turning me around to face him.

Out of breath, I huffed. 'What? What is it Jonathan?' And not knowing what he was going to do next, I nervously said, 'I can see Mulberry House from up here. Look!'

'Yes doesn't it look great? Now stay here Sofia,' he said, heading back to the car. 'Stay there, don't move!' He shouted, as he opened the car boot.

It looked as if he'd bought me a canvas. Did he want me to paint this spectacular scene? Right here, right now? But I couldn't, I hadn't brought my brushes and oils.

He ran back and handed it to me. 'I hope you like it?' He said, out of breath with a keenness that was so sincere.

Tearing at the wrapper as fast as I could, surprisingly I exclaimed, 'Lillie Langtry?! Jonathan it's beautiful - she's beautiful. You remembered?'

'Do you like it? He asked. 'I knew you would. It's to hang on your bedroom wall, to remind you every day of this great 'Wonder.'

I could see he was pleased.

'I love it…..and I love you,' I said, throwing my arms around him.

'What did you just say?' He asked, gently taking my face in his hands so I could look into his eyes.

He wanted me to say it again.

'I said…..I love you, you fool!' I screamed at the top of my voice. 'I love you Jonathan Guilbey!'

That summer in Jersey, under its sun and stars, I fell in love. I Sofia Constantine fell in love with *my* Jonathan Guilbey.

The next day I sat on the beach by myself while Jonathan and his family were in the house packing. I hated this so much; it was all so very painful and so very final having to turn my back on this beautiful place, having to leave it all behind. How would I be able to say

My first summer in Jersey, 1978.

goodbye? How could I let him go?

The tears rolled down my face as I felt the gentle touch of his hand on my shoulder. Again we were together but I couldn't look at him, I didn't want him to see me this way so I continued staring out into the ocean because I knew if I dared to look into his eyes I would lose control. He sat down beside me and cradled me in his arms and that was the moment I broke down. I couldn't hold it together anymore. I buried my face in his chest and sobbed as he held me close. I sobbed so much I thought my heart would stop.

'Please Sofia, don't cry.'

'Jonathan I can't, I can't do it. This is too painful.'

'Yes you can. You're my strong girl.'

I sobbed more with his words. 'Jonathan, you know I love you, don't you?'

'And I love you so much it hurts,' he wiped the tears from my eyes.

'Jonathan, what are we to do?' I wept.

'Shh, no more, no more now.'

Autumn, September 1978, England.

Chapter Ten

The first letter I was about to send Jonathan seemed the most difficult thing. I sat in my room with my blanket by the window overlooking the back garden where I could see Guilbey Farm. The only thing I held on to was the knowledge that with every letter I sent him I would receive one back and we would be closer to seeing one another again. I must have read it ten times over before sealing it with a kiss, it read:

Saturday, 5th September 1978

My dearest Jonathan,

This has to be the hardest letter I've ever had to write because I'm sad that I'm not with you, but also happy for having spent the most amazing two weeks of my life with you in Jersey. I hope you are well and missing me as much as I you? Nothing here at Holly Blue has changed, only that you are not at arms reach. I lay here at night on my sofa staring out into the back garden, just looking at your bedroom window knowing you're not there and my heart sinks because it misses you, your cheeky grin, that tender loving look you give me, your arms embracing me and your voice - I miss your voice. And even though we were together only last week, it feels like an eternity before we will see each other again...

There is nothing I can tell you on paper that you haven't already heard from my lips. I love you and hope you're not having too much of a good time at university without me. I've been keeping myself busy with another painting and the little art shop in the village put some of my works in their shop window, so there's still hope for me yet!

Please write to me soon. I pray you will return to me safely.

Yours always, Sofia xxxxx

Autumn, September 1978, England.

'Sofia, your papa has just called, and he would like you to visit him this weekend.'

'But mama, I promised May I'd see her at *yia'ya's*,' I sulked, quickly covering up my letter to Jonathan.

'I know Sofia, but your papa insisted,' she paused, 'What are you doing?'

'I'm just finishing off some homework.'

'Well, you best get ready. He will be here in an hour to collect you.'

'Is Mr Bradshaw not taking me?'

'No.'

'But papa never comes to the house. Why is…?'

'Please Sofia, no more questions. Please. An hour,' she snapped, closing my bedroom door behind her as she left.

I put my letter carefully in its envelope and placing it in my bag made my way down the hallway, downstairs to the sitting room where I found Christina at the piano and Irini deep in another book. I sat on the sofa by the fireplace in silence listening to Christina practicing some new songs her music teacher had played with her earlier that day. Not daring to interrupt Irini, I just sat analysing them both while they were keeping themselves busy in their own important worlds. I wanted to shout it out; I wanted so badly to tell them that I had also been busy all day writing my first and most important letter to Jonathan. I wanted to scream: I love Jonathan Guilbey at the top of my voice. But I couldn't, because if papa accidentally found out he would be so mad. Instead I said, 'guess where I'm going?'

Christina kept on playing, and Irini kept on reading. I said it again, a little louder. 'Guess where I'm going?!' But there was nothing. Neither of them stopped what they were doing, so I shouted, 'papa's coming to pick me up!'

Christina's fingers froze, and then she turned her head to look at me. Irini put down her book and looked up too. I knew I'd get a reaction with that.

'Papa is coming to the house?' Frowned Irini.

'Yes.'

'Are you sure?' Christina added.

'Mhm,' I nodded.

'When will he be here?'

Autumn, September 1978, England.

'About an hour.'

Christina put her hands up to her mouth and looked at Irini. 'Does mama know?'

'Yes.'

'Mama knows?!' Irini exclaimed.

'She was the one who told me he was coming.' I said finding great pleasure in telling them.

'I can't bare anymore rows,' she protested, un-amused with me.

'Nor me,' agreed Christina. 'Why do you think mama's allowing papa to come?'

'I don't know,' I replied. 'Who knows what mama is thinking, maybe she's had a change of heart.'

Irini turned her head and looked at me in disbelief, her face showed all the questions her mind had no answers for. She hadn't been able to accept papa's behaviour she said would never forgive him, and sticking to her word, she hadn't yet spoken to him. Christina and I watched as she carefully placed a marker in the open page closed her book and left the room. She headed for her bedroom. Up there she wouldn't have to face him.

'Hope she'll be okay?' Sighed Christina. 'I don't like all of this Sofia.'

I stood up and went over to the piano to put my arms around her. 'Don't worry she'll be fine. Move over,' I said, pushing her aside as I squeezed my bottom onto the stool beside her. She looked genuinely petrified and vulnerable, so I quickly dropped my hands onto the keys and started to 'play', if you could call what I was doing playing the piano. My fingers were dancing like crazy and my head was shaking like mad. Christina soon joined in as we began a wild duet; she was banging her little butterfly fingers down and stomping her feet with excitement. What a racket we must have been making. When our hands were tired, fingers had turned sore and we couldn't 'play' anymore, we threw our heads back in laughter!

'Oh Sofia, you do make me laugh. I do love you,' she said.

'And I love you, silly.'

'Miss Sofia, your papa is here,' said Mrs Bradshaw.

She'd entered the sitting room so quietly we didn't hear her, but could sense her presence.

We stopped laughing and I stood up, I expected Christina to get up too but her slight body turned ridged, so I gently took hold of her hand.

'Papa's here Mrs Bradshaw?' She acknowledged me with a nod and I turned to Christina and reassured her, 'come on, papa will want to see you too.'

She looked up at me, gave a cheerless smile as she got to her feet. She was such a delicate little thing. Hand in hand we walked out into the hall where we caught sight of him waiting on the little chaise-longue. Seeing us, he automatically stood up appearing very nervous and uncomfortable and my first thought was that no one should feel that way - not in their own home. He brushed himself down then opened his arms in anticipation, waiting for us to run into them. For a moment Christina and I weren't quite sure if that was the right thing to do, but then papa gave us that grin we knew so well, and all at once the barriers were down and we were running towards him, and with one single swoop we were there, where we belonged.

'My beautiful princesses,' he said, as he held us in his strong embrace. 'But where is your sister? Where is Irini?'

I dropped my gaze and looked down at the floor away from his stare 'Sofia?' He asked.

'I don't know papa.'

'Christina?'

'I think she's in her room papa.'

'Oh, I see,' he sighed solemnly. 'Are you ready Sofia?'

'Papa, can I come too?' Asked Christina.

With an uplifted reply, he said, 'well of course you can,' though I could see he was putting on a brave face looking towards the stairs. 'Go and ask your mama, then get your things.'

Letting go of him, we excitedly ran in different directions she to find mama, and I to get my things. In no time at all we were ready and heading for the front door.

'Are you not going to say goodbye?' Asked mama, as she appeared from the conservatory with Elizabeth in her arms.

'Mama of course we were,' I said, spinning around kicking myself for almost having forgotten. I felt confused and a sudden feeling of unhappiness came over me - one of disappointment and of guilt. We were torn between the two of them, mama standing on one side of the hall with Elizabeth, and Christina and I with papa on the other. But without a second thought, we let go of our bags and found ourselves in mama's tender, loving arms.

'You have a good time my sweet girls,' she whispered.

'Yes mama,' I whispered back, giving her a kiss on the cheek.

Papa looked at Elizabeth and beckoned softly, 'Elizabeth come to me, come to papa. Where are my kisses?' he said scooping her into his arms as she ran to him. Mama turned the other way as he cradled Elizabeth tightly in his arms, I could see she was crying. He got up and carried her over to where we were standing, and for a moment stood, sad and pathetic - a broken man. But mama just wiped her tears and swallowed her pride, and then she took Elizabeth off him, turned and walked away leaving him shattered.

It was awful, seeing him like this, but he knew it was all his own doing and until mama forgave him, he would be only half a man. He turned and looked at me, put his hand on my shoulder and led us to his car. It felt just like when we were little again, when the three of us would get into the back of papa's car and go for long drives to the country, but Irini was missing now and we weren't driving to the country. It saddened me to think that might never happen again. I glanced back at the house as papa started the engine. Oh how I wished Irini could have been here with us; Christina and I staring out of the car window, while Irini read her book. Then out of nowhere and as my wish had been answered, she appeared.

'Papa, stop the car!' I shouted out aloud.

'What Sofia?'

'Stop the car! It's Irini; she's running towards us.'

Papa slammed down on the brakes, and as we came to a jerky halt, he jumped out and ran towards her.

'Papa, papa!' She called, throwing her arms around him.

'Irini, Irini my girl!' He cried.

'Papa I have missed you so much.'

'And I have missed you,' he sobbed.

The tears were rolling from both their eyes.

'Can you forgive me papa?'

'No my sweet child, you have done nothing wrong. Can you forgive me for being such a fool?'

Irini fought the urge to look back at the house as she knew mama would be watching from her bedroom window, and she simply got into the car with us.

The view from papa's apartment looked outstandingly wonderful on this sunny autumn afternoon. I stared out into the distance wondering how many times Aunt Demi must have stood here in this exact spot and how many times they had been here together. I shuddered as I turned away.

'Are you okay Sofia?' Papa said, standing beside me.

'Yes. Doesn't St Paul's look amazing?'

'Yes it does. Maybe next time you should bring your canvas and oils?'

'Yes, maybe I will.'

'Can you see Big Ben?' He said, putting one arm around me as he pointed towards it. I wasn't listening to what he was saying, I was imagining him standing here with Aunt Demi, with his arm around her, maybe just before he was about to take her into the bedroom.

'Christina...Irini are you hungry?' I asked.

I really needed to get out of this place; *their* place.

'I'm starving,' answered Christina right away.

'What about you Irini?'

'I could eat; I could eat a scabby horse,' she laughed asking papa, 'are you hungry?' Willing a yes, I waited for his reply.

'Yes, I could eat a...scabby? Horse too. I think they do a good one at the little Italian restaurant down on the corner. Shall we go?' He gestured.

It was pretty late by the time we returned, and I was so mentally exhausted all I wanted was to go straight to bed. Christina joined me but Irini sat up with papa, they had a lot to talk about, a lot of catching up to do and a lot of apologising to be done. We kissed them both good night and left them there 'til the early hours.

In the morning Christina and I got up at about ten o'clock, leaving papa and Irini asleep. We got dressed and caught a bus to Camden market. I told her I'd take her to the little café where I'd been to on numerous occasions with papa for a full English breakfast. After our huge breakfast we made our way to the market where Camden came alive with shoppers and stall holders that sold everything from exotic

Autumn, September 1978, England.

fruits, fluorescent coloured platform shoes to handmade jewellery.

But for me, the aspiring artist that I was, the rows after rows of the street paintings that lined the pavements of talented unknowns was the real reason I loved returning. This was the in place to be, buzzing with people from every corner of the planet. It was amazing, so different from the little high road near where we lived in Epping.

After three hours shopping, when we'd bought everything in sight, we jumped on the bus and made our way back to the apartment. We ran to catch the lift as the doors were about to close.

'Which floor?' Asked a lady, pressing her finger on the button keeping the doors open. 'Top please,' we replied together.

'Shh baby,' she said, as the little dog in her bag gave a squeaky bark. 'Hello, I'm Mary,' she introduced herself, and the little dog gave another yelp. 'Oh and this is Missy.'

'Hello, I'm Sofia and this is my sister, Christina,' I answered politely.

But Christina was too busy to say hello, she was fussing over Missy. 'Christina, this is Mary.'

'Sorry, hello. She's so cute,' she said, looking up - taking herself away from Missy for just a second.

'Have we met before?' Asked Mary.

'No, I don't think so, but you may have met our papa, he has an apartment here. Harry Constantine,' I reminded her.

'Oh yes I know, the Greek gentleman, extremely handsome and well mannered…. Are you here on a visit?' She inquired.

I could see from her face she knew more that she let on. She knew about papa and Aunt Demi. She must have seen them here in this lift together.

'Yes, our papa doesn't live with us anymore.'

'What a pity,' she ridiculed, under her breath. 'Well, here we are.'

The lift jolted violently as it came to a stop, and as the doors opened, I quickly stepped out, as the sudden judder movement had frightened me. I said goodbye to Mary grabbing hold of Christina and heading for the apartment. When Irini opened the door I noticed papa sitting on the sofa, he was talking to Auntie Freda and his face had turned a strange shade of grey. I glanced over at Irini so I could try and make out what had happened but she was unable to say, I knew it was serious, I knew something bad had happened. As soon as papa hung

Autumn, September 1978, England.

up the receiver he stood up, slowly walked across the room and sat on the bottom step of the staircase that led upstairs. He just sat staring at the floor, then he buried his face in his hands and wept, crying like we'd never seen him do before.

'Papa! What's wrong Papa?!' I screamed. 'Papa, please tell us. Why are you crying?' 'What's happened?' Insisted Irini, as Christina broke down into tears.

'It's your *yia'ya* Elizabeth, she's gone...She's gone my princesses, she is gone my little ones,' he was crying, murmuring what sounded like spouts of a sad dirge.

I couldn't believe it. It couldn't be true. He'd seen her only a few months ago when he'd returned to Cyprus for some business and she was fine. I began to shake, as her image suddenly came to mind, I could see her sitting on her bed, plaiting her long silver hair. All we could do was hold papa and weep. I was so overwhelmed with grief for him, sad that he'd lost his *mitera*, sad that we'd never see her again and sad because it upset him like this. I felt sick and I couldn't stand to see him in pain, being punished like this. He was just a little boy, just *my* papa again.

Autumn, September 1978, Cyprus.

Chapter Eleven

Following the sudden and unexpected death of our *yia'ya* Elizabeth, I thought it only right I should join papa in Cyprus for her funeral, after all out of the three of us, it wasn't possible for Irini to go because she had not long started university and Christina was to stay behind because she was in the middle of her mock exams at school. I was also still at school, in my first year of A levels and Mrs Fairchild wasn't at all happy about me having the time off and only agreed to me going with the assumption that I'd take my school work away with me.

Stepping off the plane at Paphos Airport, I interlinked my hand with papas; I felt so protective over him, like he was my little boy and I was the *mitera*. My Uncle Kosta had come to the airport to collect us, but this time the tears were not tears of joy, but tears full with sorrow. I was actually dreading it - papa facing Auntie Freda. *Yia'ya* had become her companion since *bapou* Pedri had passed away and her death was to be a huge blow.

I sat all alone in the back, listening to papa and Uncle Kosta making small talk on the way to the village, and as the car went up the steep mountain, I held onto the door handle, closing my eyes tightly until I heard the bells of St John ringing I knew we were near.

'We are here,' said Uncle Kosta.

I leant forward to hold onto the back of papa's seat, as if by being nearer to him it would make what had happened easier to cope with, because I knew once Auntie Freda caught sight of us it wasn't going to be pleasant. We turned the corner and straight away caught sight of her running to the car, running for papa.

'Harry! Harry!' She screamed. 'Your *mitera* gone, your *mitera* gone!'

Poor papa jumped out of the car crying and screaming, embracing her in his strong arms.

'*Yadi* Harry? Why, why have I lost her?' She wailed.

'Come Freda my love, come inside,' said Uncle Kosta, trying to comfort her. He put his arm around her and gently helped her in, him on one side and papa on the other as I followed behind, watching them gently sit her down on the sofa.

'You like some tea, Sofia?' Uncle Kosta asked.

'Yes please uncle.'

Auntie Freda then turned her stare away from papa realising she'd completely ignored me and rose her arms for me to go into. 'Oh my dear child, come, *ella* Sofia. How I not see you?' Even in her grief she turned to Uncle Kosta and told him not to forget the biscuits. 'Sofia like her biscuits,' she smiled.

The next day began with my *yia'ya* Elizabeth's funeral. I felt it was a bit quick, burying a loved one within a few days of passing, but that's how it was traditionally done in Cyprus and I knew this was a very difficult time for my auntie, but I also knew that in time she would be back to being that happy, loving auntie again, the one I'd grown to love so very much.

The weather in Cyprus was still wonderful, and I didn't want to be stuck in the house by myself, so the day after the funeral, when Uncle Kosta drove papa and Auntie Freda to Paphos for some groceries, I walked the short distance to the field at the back of the house finding a shady patch under a small olive tree where I began to write another letter to Jonathan;

Thursday, 10th September 1978.

My dearest Jonathan,

I hope you are well. I'm writing to you from Cyprus. Yes, I'm here again unexpectedly and not for a happy occasion. My yia'ya Elizabeth suddenly passed away and I thought it only right to be here for papa. I only wish you and I were together sitting under this little olive tree, taking in the lovely warm Cyprus sun. Papa and I will have to stay for at least forty days, the official time of mourning. But I can't wait to come back home, I will be back for half term and I will be with you again. I love and miss you so much. I will send my letters as promised to May who will forward to you my love and she in turn will send me yours.

112

Autumn, September 1978, Cyprus.

I'm sorry my letter is short but, my papa will be returning home soon so, for now I will have to leave only my love with you.

Please write to me soon, I can't wait to hear from you.

Yours always Sofia xxxxx

I carefully folded the letter, and put it in the envelope ready to be posted on Saturday. The postman collected and delivered the mail from the village once a week from the little café, so I took it there, handing it over with the letter I'd written to Jonathan back home at Holly Blue. I knew it had been risky bringing that letter all the way to Cyprus, but I hadn't had a moment to myself before coming here.

'*Yasou,*' said a chubby lady from behind the counter.

'Oh hello, *yasou,*' I corrected myself, 'You speak English?' I asked feeling my mouth beginning to water. There was a wonderful smell of freshly baked bread, garlic, and tomatoes.

'A little,' she replied. 'Letter for England?'

She had a broad smile on her face; I could see she had a gold tooth. 'Yes.'

'It go on Saturday. Is okay?'

'Yes, okay."

'I Voula,' she said, reaching out her hand for me to shake.

'Sofia,' I replied, returning the gesture.

Her hand was warm and sweaty, and as she pulled me near, I caught a whiff of her; sweet and musky, mixed with underarm body odour.

'Sofia? Auntie Freda, she tells me about you,' she smiled, turning her entire body away from me, her grasp becoming even tighter. She picked up a packet of boiled sweets to give to me. 'For you Sofia.'

'Oh no. Thank you Voula, but I mustn't,' I said.

My papa said we weren't to take anything from anybody.

'But why? A small gift. Please... take... Please.'

'No. I mustn't.'

'Please,' she insisted.

'Okay. Thank you, you're very kind,' I said, smiling, willing her to let go.

'You are welcome,' she smiled back with gratitude, only letting go of my hand once I'd accepted her gift.

113

Autumn, September 1978, Cyprus.

When I returned to the house I noticed Uncle Kosta's car parked out by the front yard, so I ran the rest of the way wondering what goodies they had brought back for us to eat.

'Papa! Papa!' I called, running down the side entrance to where Uncle Kosta was feeding some more corn to the chickens.

'*Yasou* Sofia. Where have you been my child?' He said, looking up.

'*Yasou* Uncle Kosta. I went to the little café to send a letter.'

'To a boy?' He asked, giving me a playful wink.

'Oh no uncle, to my friend, May. Can I help you feed them?' I said, looking down, feeling slightly uncomfortable about having to lie to him.

He handed me some dried corn and I copied him; throwing it away from my feet. I loved being around the chickens, watching them pecking at the corn. Their tiny heads amusingly bobbing up and down with such enthusiasm. But with the sudden smell of fried *haloumi* coming towards us from the kitchen and the smell from the café earlier having made me hungry and I threw the rest of the corn down as quickly as I could and hurried inside to find Auntie Freda.

'*Kali'mera* Sofia,' she smiled at me.

'Good morning auntie,' I answered, giving her a kiss on the cheek, taking in the delicious smell of fried *haloumi* and eggs. She turned and glanced at me with that, '*try to speak Greek Sofia*' look, so I apologised then said, '*kali'mera* Auntie Freda. Shall I butter the toast?' I asked, wanting to lend a hand so that we could eat. I was starving!

'Good morning my princess,' said papa, planting a kiss on my cheek.

'*Kali'mera* papa,' I replied, giving Auntie Freda a smile. 'I'm making toast,' I said.

'I can see. Don't burn your fingers.'

'Okay,' I continued, thinking I was doing something really great as I placed another slice of bread on the griddle; I'd never made toast this way before.

'Have you just got up?' He asked.

'No papa. I wrote a letter, to May and then I went to the café and posted it. I met Voula she's very nice. She gave me these,' I said, taking out the bag of sweets from my pocket to show him.

'A letter to May?'

'Yes,' I nodded trying not to make eye contact with him. I knew that if I did, he would know I was lying; he'd be able to see it on my

114

face. 'All done Auntie. I'll fetch Uncle Kosta,' I said.

I wanted to get out of the kitchen before he asked me anymore questions, so I walked quickly past him, but I could feel his stare following me out. *'Oh no, he knew,'* I thought, he somehow knew I was lying and knowing him I knew he would not let it drop. He would try and find out the truth and I would be punished. And when we'd finished eating, that's when he did it, that's when he dropped the bombshell on me saying he would be leaving for England after the forty days of mourning and that he had decided I should stay for a while longer: to keep auntie company 'til she felt better, he said. No amount of rebellion or logical reasoning was going to change his mind, I hated him. I hated him for making decisions for me, for making decisions that only took his own feelings into consideration and not mine. He'd made up his mind and that's how it would be.

When the forty days had come to an end I stood with Auntie Freda waving him goodbye with tears streaming down my face. As soon as the car was out of sight I ran upstairs to write yet another unanswered letter to Jonathan, explaining to him what had happened. I'd left it 'til now to write, hoping, upon hope, that papa would somehow have taken pity on me and allowed me to return home with him, but alas he hadn't. Forty days turned into three months, then six, and as Auntie Freda regained her strength, I lost mine. Having not one of my many letters answered, I found myself confused, and unable to understand why he had forgotten me, and why his 'undying love' had been all but a lie. I was even coming round to the idea that papa had been right all along about Jonathan, and that perhaps leaving me here was actually for the best.

I tried so desperately to get Jonathan out of my mind and out of my most intimate thoughts, but it was extremely difficult, for as much as I hated admitting it to myself, I was still very much in love with him. I swapped sitting under the willow tree at the back of our garden for the little olive tree in the field at the back of Auntie Freda's as the place I'd go to when painting a *'great masterpiece'*. Although, as time went by it progressively began to get easier and less complicated.

'Can I sit down cousin?' I heard someone say from behind the little tree.

'Andreas!' I cried.

Autumn, September 1978, Cyprus.

'Sorry. I should not have startled you Sofia.'

I couldn't believe it Andreas was here, standing in front of me; I was stuck for words. I was shaking but I didn't know why. Then from a hidden depth came laughter, I was laughing so much I didn't know if it was a laugh of relief, however what I did know is that it was a laugh that was well over due. A laugh much needed and I didn't know why it was happening, but I laughed and I laughed and he laughed humorously at and with me.

Easter, April 1979, Cyprus.

Chapter Twelve

There was a knock at the front door; Andreas had come to collect me. He'd arranged a special day - a surprise for my seventeenth birthday. The past six months here with him had been delightful, not a dull moment had been spent. The grey cloud that had cast its shadow over me had now been lifted and blown away. I found falling in love with Andreas very easy. How could I not, for he turned out to be the sweetest, most generous man I could ever dream of. I had, in the beginning, only wanted to be friends, to be cousins, but he had other ideas in mind and he wasn't going to let me slip from his hold, from his strong and loving arms - not as Jonathan had done!

With one arm on the steering wheel and the other around my shoulder holding me close, Andreas drove up Troodos Mountain and he knew from past experience that mountains frightened the living daylights out of me, so he needed no reminding not to go too fast. With the radio on full blast, we sang to our favourite songs. It was his way of calming me down as the car climbed higher and higher.

'Troodos Mountain!' Oh what a beautiful place, the powerful aroma coming from their graceful authority was to die for. Andreas promised he would bring me here one day with my canvas and oils to capture their beauty in a painting to hang on a wall in our house, to remind us everyday of the place where we fell in love. An uncanny thought being as Lillie hung there at the moment.

I was so full of anticipation. 'What have you got for me?' I asked, as Andreas parked the car. He looked over at me with a smile repeating, 'it is a surprise my love.'

I both loved and loathed surprises and because I knew he wasn't going to tell me I reluctantly gave up my plea and instead began taking out the contents of the boot. Was there nothing he hadn't packed? There was absolutely everything, food and drink, a tent that would be our home for the night and some logs for a fire.

Easter, April 1979, Cyprus.

'Now, sit yourself down. You will do nothing but eat and drink,' he said. 'And I will be at your beckoned call.' He bowed his head and gave me a wave of his hand.

His gesture reminded me of my time in Jersey with Jonathan and I think Andreas must have detected something had upset me because straight away he asked, quietly concernedly if I was okay.

'Yes, everything's fine, Andreas,' I replied, throwing my arms around him so he couldn't see my eyes welling.

I was about to burst into tears and I wouldn't have been able to hide or explain that. I wasn't sure where these feelings had suddenly surfaced from but I wanted them to go away. So I held onto him for a moment, trying hard to pull myself together but I couldn't shake the vision of Jonathan's cheeky grin, nor his seductive stare teasing me.

'Happy birthday, Sofia,' Andreas whispered, kissing my cheek.

'Thank you for my beautiful day,' I said back, my face touching his.

'No, thank you,' he said, running his fingers through my hair, and without letting go, he gently and playfully twisted the strands, making the hairs on the back of my neck stand up.

'What for?' I asked, not being able to move as his touch was hypnotizing me.

'For being here, for being you and for making me happy. Are you happy Sofia?'

'Yes,' I smiled.

'Then close your eyes.'

'Why?'

'Close them!'

I could hear him rattling around; he then took hold of my hand and gently placed something on my wrist.

'Open!' He said. 'Happy birthday!'

'Oh Andreas!' I cried. 'Andreas it's charming.'

'A bracelet made especially for you, with your favourite butterfly.'

'It's beautiful,' I said, admiringly studying its delicate blue wings.

'Is it the right one Sofia? The Holly Blue?' He asked.

'It's perfect - so perfect - just as you are Andreas.'

'Good, because that is all I want for us, to be happy, to be like we are right now forever.'

'Me too.'

Easter, April 1979, Cyprus.

'*Sa'ya'po* Sofia,' he said. 'I love you very much and I - I would like to ask you...'

'What is it? What do you want to ask me Andreas?'

'I know it is what everyone is expecting but I want to ask you anyway. I want to hear it from your lips Sofia, make me the happiest man alive - marry me?!'

My face lit up as I let out a cry and without a second thought I accepted his proposal.

'Yes! Yes I will! Of course I will!' I screamed.

With that he pulled me onto him, his gentle kisses slowly turning into ones of intense desire. We were alone here on our mountain, in our tent, in our own special world. I wanted him to make love to me and my body told him so. Yet I knew he was a little hesitant for he knew I'd never been alone with a man before and he wanted to be sure, be very careful not to make a mistake. I looked at his face, into his eyes and that's when it all started to happen, there under the moon and the stars, in between the aromatic pines as they protectively bowed over us shielding us from the outside world. He rolled me onto my back unbuttoning the front of my dress, exposing my body for only him to see and only him to touch.

'Andreas,' I sighed breathlessly.

'Sofia, Sofia.' He repeated, his lips so gentle on my dampened skin.

Running my hands through his hair then down his back, feeling the sweat, feeling the heat from his body on mine I groaned as he pressed down on me, lifting my already arched body to his, it felt so natural, finally becoming one.

In the morning I woke lying in his arms and my first reaction was to cover up my naked body. He was still sleeping, looking so peaceful and content that I didn't want to wake him, but as I tried quietly to get up he gave a blissful groan and pulled me back to him, back for more - I didn't resist; I let him make love to me again.

When we eventually returned to the village Auntie Freda greeted us with a huge grin. I was so embarrassed because it was so obvious she knew, it was written all over her face. She knew about last night and she probably knew about this morning too. I tried keeping cool but it was all in vain because I almost certainly must have had it written all

Easter, April 1979, Cyprus.

over my face. I was seventeen and now a woman; a woman, what a laugh! An unashamedly, beautiful woman!

A few weeks before 'the day' March 1983.

Chapter Thirteen

As time went by Jonathan couldn't have been further from my mind and for the first time I was happy and content since leaving Jersey. Happy with my life here in Cyprus and just being in love with Andreas. It was coming up to my fifth year away from home and I had nearly finished university. Andreas had made sure I had attended an English school when I first arrived, telling papa '*only the best will do.*' Papa had happily agreed to pay for the privilege and with my degree nearly coming to an end, I would soon be an art graduate. I was quite surprised how time had flown by so quickly and I was to become twenty one on my next birthday, Andreas and I would be married and we would be living in the house papa had built for us.

It was nothing unusual for a Greek girl to be married by the time she was twenty one, and although my life was now in Cyprus, I always dreamt of getting married at home in England with all my family around me. Andreas was aware of that, and promised we would be on the next flight out as soon as university was over. I couldn't wait! I would be wearing my beautiful white wedding dress, marrying my handsome 'prince', with Christina playing the piano. Oh! How I missed listening to her playing whilst I sat in the sitting room with dear Irini reading her book. Not a single day went by when I wouldn't think of them both, and of my mama, *yia'ya* Athena and baby sister, Elizabeth. I hadn't seen them for two long years, not since the last time mama brought them over for a holiday.

'Mama has booked the wedding Andreas! April seventeenth, my birthday. Isn't that just fab!?' I announced coming off the phone from my mama. I was excited, even though it wasn't my Christmas wedding.

'Fab!' He laughed, lifting me up into the air. 'Only a true princess gets married on her birthday.'

'Stop it! You're embarrassing me.'

'You? Embarrassed? Never my love, I do not believe you,' he said, as I turned a ruby red. 'I am not making you blush, am I?'

A few weeks before 'the day' March 1983.

'No,' though I could feel my cheeks burning.

'I will make you blush for real,' he teased, giving me a kiss.

'I'm sure you will,' I smirked, then turned calling for Auntie Freda. 'Andreas is here! We have some good news!'

'What news my children?' She said, wiping her hands on her apron as she came towards us from the kitchen.

'Andreas, you tell auntie.'

'Tell me what?' She beamed.

'Sofia and I are to be married, April seventeenth, on her....'

'*Yineth'lia* - her birthday!' She added excitedly. 'That is wonderful! That is wonderful!' She cried, embracing us both in her arms. 'This is so happy? Yes?!'

'Yes,' we said in unison.

'Good. I will go tell Uncle Kosta.'

'Let us go and tell my parents, Sofia,' Andreas said, taking hold of my hand. 'They will be so thrilled.'

It was late by the time we returned to auntie's, and because Andreas had an early flight to Greece in the morning, he walked me to the front door and kissed me goodnight. I stood on the porch watching as he got into his car and drove off. Letting out a contented sigh I turned around and went inside, hoping Auntie Freda would be up waiting with a cup of tea for a girly chat. But she didn't run to greet me and I thought she'd already gone to bed so I switched off the lamps in the hall and locked the door, that's when I noticed the light still on in the sitting room.

I hurriedly made my way to find her. 'Auntie, are you up?' I called out. When I entered the room I saw her sitting on the sofa, she had an odd, worried look on her face and I began to feel extremely uneasy. I'd had enough shocking news in my life and I wasn't sure I could take any more. So, quickly walking over to her I noticed a letter in her hand. 'What is it auntie?' I asked, looking down at her lap.

'A letter from England,' she answered slowly, staring down at it.

'Auntie?' I said anxiously hoping it wasn't from my mama.

'Is for you Sofia. It has your name on it.' There was a silence, a long and dragging silence and then she looked at me. 'Please sit down Sofia. Is letter from Margaret, Margaret Guilbey,' she said, handing it over. I took it from her and suddenly my hands were shaking. I quickly tore it open, it read:

A few weeks before 'the day' March 1983.

Thursday 4th March, 1983.

My dear Sofia,

How are you? We heard you'd left England and we hope you have been happy living in Cyprus. We have been well, nothing much has changed - it never does!

Jonathan graduated from university and is now working as a lawyer, we are very proud, and Sarah is enjoying her first year at college studying fashion design. Uncle Henry still potters about the farm keeping him busy and Grandma Guilbey is as well as can be expected.

I am though unfortunately writing to you with the sad news that Aunt Vi passed away last night and I thought it only right you should know. Her funeral will be held in Jersey, on Friday 12th March.

I'm so sorry to be the bearer of such sad news, but I'm sure you would have wanted to be told. Take care lovey.

Love and kisses Aunt Margi x

I sat on the sofa staring at the letter until the words were not words anymore, just blurry shapes, and the pain I was feeling was so real and deep I was finding it hard to fight back the tears.

'I must leave for Jersey tomorrow,' I murmured, without lifting my head. 'This letter is dated the fourth and the funeral's this Friday.'

'Sofia, no my child you cannot. You be getting married soon, just over one month. There is still so much to do and so little time.'

'Auntie this is important. I must go.' I replied, looking straight into her eyes, she could see the tears rolling down my face and could see how upset I was.

'Your dress fitting Sofia,' she pleaded, 'so little time,' her desperation willing me not to go.

'I must call Andreas and let him know,' I said, heading for the telephone. It seemed like the moment I put down the receiver Andreas appeared at the front door, he swiftly entered the house past Auntie Freda.

'Is there a problem, my love?' Andreas asked; his voice trembling.

'Do you remember I told you about Aunt Vi who lived in Jersey? Andreas, she's passed away. I must go to the funeral?' I panicked. 'It's

123

A few weeks before 'the day' March 1983.

only right.'

'When?'

'Straight away I'm afraid. The funeral's on Friday.'

'Have you told your papa?' He shamelessly asked, knowing too well that if my papa was informed he would not allow me to go.

'No. There is no need. Please don't tell him,' I pleaded, taking hold of his hand, entwining his fingers in mine.

'Sofia are you sure that is all? There is nothing else you want to tell me?' He said, bringing my hand up to his lips as he began to kiss it.

His questioning suddenly jerked the thought of Jonathan to my mind. 'There's nothing else. There's nothing for you to worry about,' I said reassuringly looking into his eyes, though it was I who needed the reassurance. But there was something else and I had to get to the bottom of it. I had letters unanswered, there were questions I needed to ask and Jonathan was the only one who could answer them.

Uncle Kosta drove us to the newly built Paphos Airport and with my ticket in order and suitcase checked in, I said my goodbyes to Andreas. I tried not to let the desperate look on his face twist my guilt, 'I won't be long. I'll be back, I promise.' I walked straight through passport control without turning to look at him as I knew my promises were disbelieved.

Nearly five hours and some turbulence later the plane landed safely at Heathrow Airport, I was so glad to be back on the ground. I looked out of the tiny window and the first thing I noticed were the grey clouds, drizzling rain with the sun fighting its way through. The captain thanked us for flying *Cyprus Airways* wishing us a pleasant stay, hoping we would fly with them again. I looked down at my watch, it was four o'clock, and I had two hours 'til I would be boarding a flight to Jersey - to Jonathan!

The clouds had now given way and the drizzle had stopped, but as I boarded the tiny plane not even the warm rays from the sun could stop me from shaking.

'Are you cold Miss?' Asked the very pretty hostess.

'Yes, a little,' I looked up, her question wrenching me away from my thoughts.

'I'll get you a blanket,' she smiled.

A few weeks before 'the day' March 1983.

In one swift moment, she'd returned with my blanket, I clicked my safety belt together and covered up. 'Thanks,' I smiled back.

'You're welcome,' she replied, and then robotically noticing another passenger in need of assistance, she was gone.

With the plane now speeding down the runway for takeoff I shut my eyes tightly, by the expression on my face nobody would have ever guessed I wanted to be a hostess when I was a young girl - a dream in which papa had put a stop to from the moment it had been suggested. *'How and who will you marry if you're forever in the sky?'* he'd said, because that's all he ever dreamt about, talked about and thought about - who we were going to marry, how many children we were going to have and where we were going to live? How on earth could he keep a watch over us if we were not at arms reach? Travelling the world was out of the question!

When I opened my eyes I found myself sitting next to a little old lady dressed in a pink and lavender floral outfit with a row of pearls sitting tightly round her chubby neck. She reminded me of Grandma Guilbey minus the whiskers and my *yia'ya* Athena minus the rosy smelling perfume. I smiled at her hoping her friendly face would calm my nerves and I found myself wondering who she was visiting in Jersey. Maybe she was visiting her son or daughter? Maybe it was an equally old brother or sister? Or perhaps a long lost love she'd not seen for years? And as she returned my smile I held onto the warm comforting thought that it *was* her long lost love she was visiting.

Keeping her warm smile with me I turned away and glanced out of the tiny egg-shaped window, where all I could see were the rooftops of thousands of houses - so small and so perfectly placed looking like a mini Lego-land. As the land below gradually turned into a huge oddly shaped chequer board of green and yellow farmland, I knew it would not take long for the flight to be over and all too soon the captain would be wishing us yet another pleasant stay.

As soon I stepped out of the airport I hailed down the first cab I saw which screeched to a halt in front of me, the cabby jumped out to open my door. I climbed into the back asking him to take me to The Victoria hotel which overlooked the sea in St Helier.

'Done!' He said shutting my door.

A few weeks before 'the day' March 1983.

I sat in silence as we zoomed along the coast and staring out of the window at the ocean I felt the wind as it travelled freely in my hair and all at once I could smell sugared doughnuts. The Queen Elizabeth castle suddenly came into view, becoming larger and larger as we quickly approached our destination and as the cabby made another sudden halt, I turned my head to see The Victoria - its delightfulness took my breath away - it was charming.

'Can you please pick me up tomorrow?' I asked before getting out.

'Yes luv. What time?' He turned around to face me.

'Ten o'clock. Is that okay?'

'Done!'

'Thank you,' I replied. 'How much do I owe you?' I took my purse out from my handbag to pay him the fare.

'That'll be three quid luv.'

I handed over five and told him to keep the change.

'Thanks luv,' he said, accepting my generosity. 'See you in the morning. Who shall I ask for luv?'

'Sofia.... Sofia Constantine,' I replied.

I got out of the car and stood for a moment motionless, taking in the quaintness of this wonderfully charming house-turned-hotel.

I heard the car's tyres shriek as the cabby sped off.

It had been a very long day but I'd made it; I was in Jersey and I hadn't missed Aunt Vi's funeral. I knew Andreas would much rather I hadn't come, especially knowing Jonathan would also be here. Maybe I'd been too honest with him when we first met, maybe I should have kept Jonathan to myself, but Andreas had nothing to worry about.

'*I was well and truly over Jonathan Guilbey,*' I reassured myself, but upon entering my beautiful room, I slumped down on the neatly made double bed and wasn't sure that was all together true, for my mind began spinning, jumping from one daydream to another, the main occupant being Jonathan. Confused I began to panic thinking about tomorrow; I needed to sleep to clear my head so I decided to have shower, but as soon as I turned it on the telephone rang.

'Hello,' said a man's voice.

'Hello. Who's this?' I answered, not recognising him straight away.

'Have you forgotten me already, my love?'

'Andreas!'

A few weeks before 'the day' March 1983.

'Who were you expecting?'

'No one my love. How are you?' I quickly said.

'I am fine except missing you,' he replied, there was concern in his tone.

'And I'm missing you too. What's been happening whilst I've been away? I asked as though I'd been gone from Cyprus for more than a few hours.

'Nothing my love, for time stands still when you are not near.' He sighed

'Oh, Andreas, don't be sad I cannot bare to think of us so far apart. I feel as I'm on the other side of the planet, but I'll be home in a few days.' I reassured him.

'Make sure to be,' he said

'Please let Auntie Freda and Uncle Kosta know I'm okay and tell them not to worry. I do love you.' I reassured him. 'I'll speak to you tomorrow,' I said and hung up keeping his loving words with me.

Unbuttoning my blouse and skirt and letting them both drop to the floor, I was going to skip showering though the sound of the water splashing to the ground sounded so inviting. I closed my eyes as I stepped into the warmth of the trickling water, letting it first stroke my face then my body, allowing it to run away and letting my mind go with it 'til all I could feel was Andreas' hands seductively caressing me, travelling freely and knowingly wanting only to please. Andreas kissed my lips then my neck, touched my body in a way he only knew how. I let out a gentle moan but it wasn't he who'd come into my mind, Jonathan was there instead.

Ten o'clock the next morning the cabby was waiting for me in the hotel reception as promised.

'Morning Miss Constantine,' he said.

'Morning,' I politely replied.

'Where are we off to?'

'Mulberry House, on Mulberry Hill please. But could you first stop at the nearest florist?' I said getting into the cab

'Oh, very nice. Do you have family here?'

'Yes, well sort of.'

A few weeks before 'the day' March 1983.

'Have they lived in Jersey long? I've lived here all my life. Born and bred. Are you from Jersey?'

'No. No I'm not.'

'Where are you from luv?' He asked, carrying on with his questioning.

'Epping, Essex in England.'

'Here on holiday?'

'No. A funeral I'm afraid,' I answered quickly, hoping he would stop asking more questions.

'Oh, I'm sorry luv,' he said. And for the rest of the journey he didn't say anymore - not until we got to Aunt Vi's anyway. He courteously parked his cab outside the house and got out to open my door, kindly reaching out his hand.

'You okay luv?' He asked.

'Yes thanks. You're very kind...How much do I owe you?'

'Just call it a fiver luv.'

'Are you sure?'

'Yes that's more than enough.'

'Well thank you. You're the nicest cabby I've ever met; do you have a business card? Please take seven,' I said, handing him a ten pound note.

'Thanks luv and yes I do,' he replied, as he began rummaging in a little pouch, and then pulling one out, he smiled and said, 'I knew they were at the bottom somewhere, here we are.'

'Well, thank you again. Goodbye.' I took the little card and turned towards the house.

'Bye luv,' he replied.

The front door at Aunt Vi's was wide open and the pathway leading to it was overflowing with bouquets, wreaths and beautifully arranged flowers. Violet and white dominated this normally beautifully coloured garden. Violet and white, quite appropriate I thought. I carefully laid my bouquet of lilies down on the ground and with my mind still bursting with thoughts of last night I walked into the house.

I entered the sitting room where everybody was dressed in black, it was quite difficult to make out who was who but I spotted Sarah sitting on the window-seat, she was holding Mittens. I quickly went over to say hello and her quick response was to push Mittens off and run straight to me.

A few weeks before 'the day' March 1983.

'Hello Sarah,' I said, taking her into my arms. 'I'm so very sorry about Aunt Vi.'

'Thanks Sofia. I'm glad you're here. Aunt Vi would have been glad too,' she said emotion running high in her voice.

I'd never seen her upset before. She seemed all grown up now and not at all that same little girl I'd spent two weeks with so long ago.

'Yes I know she would, and that's why I'm here,' I replied.

'Oh Sofia, we've missed you so much. Jonathan's missed you too. How long are you staying for?'

My mind fell silent for a moment, 'I've missed you all too but I'm afraid I'll be gone straight after the funeral. I'm returning to England for a few days, to Holly Blue before returning back home.' It felt strange to think of Cyprus as home. 'Where's Aunt Margaret and Uncle Henry? I must say hello,' I said, looking around the room.

'Don't you want to say hello to me?' Asked a voice that I'd longed to hear all these years.

'Jonathan!' I said, spinning to face him.

'Hello Sofia.'

I'd been anticipating seeing him from the moment I'd read Aunt Margaret's letter, from the moment I'd stepped off the plane here in Jersey and from the moment I'd entered Aunt Vi's. I suddenly felt a little light headed but I managed to pull myself together, just enough to calmly say hello.

'How are you?' He asked, uncomfortably pulling at his collar. 'I hate wearing these shirts,' he added.

'I'm okay. You?'

I could see the tension in his stare, I knew him well enough to know all he wanted was to lift me up into his arms and kiss me.

'I've been busy in the real world, working....' And without warning, he stopped making small talk and asked.... 'Why didn't you write to me Sofia?'

'I did! I wrote to you. You didn't reply.' But just as I was about to tell him what I thought of him, Uncle Henry cut in.

'Hello everybody,' he said. 'My dear wife Margaret and I would like to welcome you all on this sad day to celebrate the life, not death, of our very own Aunt Vi. I'm sure she would have hated to see you all upset. So please let us greet her and welcome her home for the very last

129

time...Thank you.'

'You wrote to me?' Jonathan said in disbelief.

'Yes. I wrote for six months,' I answered quietly as we started making our way outside.

'I didn't get your letters Sofia!' he said, taking hold of my arm pulling me back.

'Keep your voice down!' I snapped. 'Everybody's staring at us.' Aunt Vi's cortège was waiting and I turned to look at him hoping he would stop it. 'Not now Jonathan. Not here,' I whispered firmly trying to pull away from his hold.

'When?' He said, refusing to let go 'til I gave him my reply.

'Meet me tomorrow at one o'clock, on Mulberry Hill.'

It was a small family funeral, a very private affair, only immediate relatives and friends had been invited. Aunt Vi had been a colourful character and was well loved by everyone who'd ever met her. I sat and listened to the priest talk about the great woman she was and all the good work she'd voluntarily done for her favourite charity, The Widows of War - a subject that was close to her heart. Sarah and Jonathan each read out a prayer from the Holy Bible and the choir sang Aunt Vi's favourite songs - ones that she'd chosen just before she died - and at Aunt Vi's request, she was then to be cremated and her ashes scattered at her home in her back garden overlooking the sea. How romantic and at the same time how tragic, I thought, that Aunt Vi's ashes should be scattered at the very place where she would sit for hours looking out at sea, wondering when her love would return to her. She had given her heart away a long time ago to an army officer, only to lose him to war. She'd given her heart away once and never again; she'd told me this when we'd first met, *once had been enough,*' she'd said.

Her tragic, yet fairytale life reminded me of papa's beginning. The year 1946 was unforgettable for both of them. Harry was on his way to Paphos, crying on the bus, twelve years old with his world having just fallen apart, Violet was nearly three thousand miles away in Jersey still mourning the death of her fiancé, a year after he'd died. He was just twenty two years old - a wasted life that stopped hers beginning. At least papa didn't let his break him.

Theirs was yet another tragic love story doomed, as was that of

A few weeks before 'the day' March 1983.

Anthony and Cleopatra, Romeo and Juliet, Heathcliff and Cathy. Even at the tender age of eighteen, Violet Hemming, a rare beauty, knew about love. She'd seen enough films on the subject and read enough books, and as far as she was concerned, she knew it all. She knew who she was going to fall in love with, and when.

Alfred Jonathan Wallis, a dashing young officer caught her eye. Dressed in full uniform, he'd entered The Grand Hall and within no time two giggling girls were on either arm. Leading them to the dance floor they danced all night 'til they'd became so dizzy he had no choice but to leave with them both. Most men would have been happy going home with just one pretty girl on his arm, but not Alfred! That's when Violet decided she was going to have him and that she would tame and keep him for herself - and tame him she did. They fell head over heels in love; nothing and no one were going to get in their way. How young, innocent and naive they had been, for ten months later, Alfred Jonathan Wallis was killed in battle and her heart was broken, never to be mended again.

*　　*　　*　　*　　*　　*　　*　　*　　*

The next morning I found my kind cabby sitting in the reception of the hotel waiting for me. I'd asked him to pick me up at twelve o'clock because I had a flight to England at three o'clock that afternoon, but he was to first take me to meet Jonathan.

As soon as he saw me, he put down his newspaper and stood. 'Hello Sofia. You don't mind if I call you Sofia?' He asked.

'Hello Peter, no of course not. Thank you for coming.'

'How was the funeral? Not too bad I hope?' He remembered taking my suitcase off me as we headed for his cab.

'It was sad but at the same time beautiful, thanks for asking.' I smiled an instant reaction to his that was so genuine and sincere - I felt completely at ease talking to him. I don't know why but sometimes you just connect with certain people and he was definitely one of those people. He opened the cab door for me and after putting my luggage in the boot we were off.

'Where to Sofia luv?'

'Mulberry Hill, please.'

131

A few weeks before 'the day' March 1983.

'Okay luv. Done!'

I sat in silence, staring out at the fantastic view of the vast ocean and it was limitless just like the love Jonathan and I had once felt for one another. I wondered what he would say or do once we were alone again, on the hill I'd first told him I loved him. I was excited at the thought of seeing him, at the thought of us being alone. The butterflies in my stomach had once again begun to stir, making me feel a little ill. I knew what I was doing was wrong and suddenly I couldn't rid the enormous guilty feeling that now clouded my thoughts. I couldn't think of anyone but Andreas and how he loved and trusted me enough to let me be here. I'm not sure if it had been the same the other way around that I would have been so generously trusting. I turned my stare away from the ocean and looked down at my ring that I had accepted from Andreas as a symbol of our love, it said, *'I belonged only to him'*.

'Peter stop! Stop the cab please!' I called out to him.

'Sorry luv. Did you say something?'

'Yes! Please stop!'

'What's the matter luv?' He asked, trying to find a safe place where he could pull over.

'This is wrong. Please could you just take me to the airport?'

'Are you okay luv?'

'Yes. I've made a mistake. Please I must go to airport,' I repeated worried if he didn't do it right away I might change my mind I hadn't come to do this, I'd come for answers and answers alone, answers that I need not know- not now.

'Are you sure?'

'Yes.' I said, or at least my head was saying so.

'It's to the airport then,' he said and carefully turned the cab around.

When we got there I felt as though I was saying goodbye to an old acquaintance. He took hold of my hand giving it a firm sincere shake, 'you take care, and any time you're back in Jersey,' he said.

'Yes, I'll be sure to call you. Thanks,' I smiled.

I took my luggage off him and entered the airport through the sliding doors. As they closed behind me I looked back but Peter had already gone and I wasn't sure if we'd ever meet again.

It was early evening by the time I arrived home and Holly Blue looked

A few weeks before 'the day' March 1983.

incredible. I'd almost forgotten what a splendid house it was. What a surprise I was about to spring on everyone. I couldn't wait to see their faces. I rang the door bell hoping Christina and Irini would be running, fighting to open it but there was no sign of them, there was nothing but total darkness. So I made my way to the back of the house by the side entrance. The wooden side door would be locked but papa always kept a spare key for the padlock and one for the summerhouse under the little rockery in between the hedgerows. As soon as I entered the garden the flood lights automatically came on helping me find my way.

Hurriedly, I made my way down the crazy-paved pathway towards the summerhouse, where I'd have to stay 'til mama returned home. The hinges gave a squeaky sound as I pushed open the door, and as I entered the half darkened room I automatically locked the door before switching on the side lamps. I glanced over at the sofa and with one single blink I could see them together - laughing as papa stroked Aunt Demi's hair. I took a deep breath and sighed out a million thoughts.

Then without getting undressed I pulled back the blanket and fell onto the sofa. I couldn't have been sleeping for more that a couple of hours when I was woken by the pounding sound of the rain as it came crashing down hard and fierce on the glass roof. Papa used to love the sound and whenever it rained he would either sit in the conservatory or come out here. I turned up the radio and pulled the covers over my head just like when I was small and afraid. 'Please stop,' I said to myself.

But the tapping was getting stronger and louder. 'Sofia! Open the door! Sofia!' It was howling. I closed my eyes even tighter as I put my hands over my ears. The wind and the rain were trying to get in and they weren't having any of it.

'Sofia! Sofia!' It called again. I could feel the anxiety building; my heart was jumping from my chest. Panic was setting in, though I must know this voice as it clearly knew my name; knew I was there.

I threw back the cover and let out an enormous loud relieved scream, 'JONATHAN!' I yelled, not giving my feet time to touch the floor I ran and opened the door. 'JONATHAN!' I yelled again, flinging my arms around him. Then letting my arms drop from around his neck I took a step back from him and slowly asked, 'why are you here?'

He didn't answer he just glanced down at me as if he could see right through me, as if he knew what I'd been wishing.

A few weeks before 'the day' March 1983.

'You're soaked right through. Get these clothes off,' I continued, helping him with his jacket.

'Why didn't you meet me in Jersey?' He asked, taking hold of my hands.

'Because I didn't,' I shrugged not having an obvious answer.

'Just like you didn't write?'

'Stop it,' I said trying to help him with his jacket - it was drenched.

'Sofia why didn't you write?' He repeated.

Frustrated by his repetitions I shouted back, 'I did!'

'Am I supposed to believe you? I'll ask you again. Why didn't you meet me on Mulberry Hill?' He sounded back.

'Because!'

'Because? Because you don't love me? Because you never did? Tell me Sofia I need to know!'

'I DID LOVE YOU!...I've always loved you!'

'So why didn't you write?'

'I did! I wrote for six months. I wrote but you never wrote back. I hadn't forgotten you, I never stopped loving you!'

'I didn't get your letters Sofia! Not one! Did you think it was over for me? Did you?!... I've loved you from the moment I saw you and I still love you now!' He took hold of me pulling me to him just as he'd done so many times in Jersey and so many times my dreams. Only this time his grasp was more intense, more powerful and his stare so piercing that our bodies again were one, we began to tremble at the thought of what was about to happen. 'So if this feeling is the truth why didn't you meet me at Mulberry Hill Sofia?'

My eyes dropped from his tender loving gaze and, I sighed, regretfully 'Because....because I have a fiancé.'

'What?!'

'A fiancé!'

'You can't have.'

'I have! That's why I didn't meet you Jonathan, that's why!'

'Is that the only reason?' He said his face so close I could feel his trembling lips on mine.

'Yes!'

'Do you still love me?' He asked, but there was a pause and he asked me again. 'Sofia? Do you still love me?'

134

A few weeks before 'the day' March 1983.

'Yes,' I whispered as a single tear fell down my cheek.

Momentarily we fell tenderly into each others arms, but this moment was far over due and without a second thought we were tearing at each others clothes, pulling and ripping them off. He kissed my lips and picking me up into his arms he carried me to the sofa. I could feel his heart thumping in his chest as I wrapped myself around him, tasting the sweetness that was coming from his mouth into mine. I wanted him, longed for him and now there was no turning back. With his throbbing body on mine his hands began to race finding their way to where I wanted them to be 'til I gave myself to him willingly. So beautifully we made love 'til we fell asleep exhausted in each others embrace.

There was a calm stillness in the air now that the wind and rain had finally left us in peace, and with the sun's rays surrounding us it left a warm glow inside of me. I could have happily lay, watching him sleep forever; last night he had shown me the true meaning of love.

'Jonathan. Are you sleeping? Wake up,' I kissed his forehead, his eyes, and his full, sensual lips.

He gave me a satisfied moan and then smiled, 'you can have more of me later.'

'I want you now,' I jested, playfully teasing him as I caressed his body with mine.

Taking hold of my hand he guided it down his sleek body making me aware of his aroused state. 'Now look what you've done,' he said, 'kiss me, kiss me, me lady.'

'Now it is then,' I said.

After our fruitful evening and early morning tease we began to feel hungry and Jonathan suggested we go to the farm, reminding me that my family would soon be returning. We quickly got dressed and tidied up leaving no trace of us having ever been there.

'I'll make us something to eat there,' he kissed me, giving me a prompt reminder of the spectacular love making of last night and of this morning.

We locked the door of the summerhouse behind us and made our way to the bottom of the garden where we jumped over the fence, running like crazy through the over grown grass towards the chickens and geese. Suddenly I was back to when I'd run like this without a care in the world

A few weeks before 'the day' March 1983.

with my sisters and May playing 'hide and seek.' I turned to look behind me at Jonathan as he followed and guiding him to the first little chicken shed we were approaching, I stopped at the exact spot where he'd surprised me on my birthday with a kiss.

I took hold of his hand as I drew him closer. Now it was I who was kissing him, 'Jonathan,' I sighed, 'what are we going to do?'

'About what?'

'Us.'

'What about us?' he replied, laying me down on the ground as he began to unbutton my blouse.

'I have a fiancé back in Cyprus waiting for me.'

He stopped and looked straight at me, 'then you'll call him and tell him it's over, you're not going back,' he said casually as if Andreas meant nothing.

'Jonathan it's not as easy as that!' I replied, tugging him off me swiftly getting to my feet as I hurriedly made my way to the farmhouse.

'Wait Sofia, stop!' He called, standing up to chase after me. 'Sofia wait! You're not actually thinking of going back?!'

'I have to!' I stopped to face him.

'You don't!' he frowned, his eyes questioning me, willing me to agree with him.

'He's my fiancé for God's sake! I'm getting married in a few weeks!' I screamed.

'But you're here now with me!' He shouted.

'He asked me to marry him, I accepted, it's not that simple! He loves me!' I shouted back trying to control my tears.

'I'm in love with you! Does that mean nothing?!' He yelled.

'Yes it does, of course it does, but I gave him my word,' my whole body shook.

'You just made love to me. You told me you never stopped loving me. Did it all mean nothing to you Sofia?'

'I have to go,' I said.

'I went through a roller coaster of emotions when I thought I'd lost you, when I thought I might never see you again.'

'I have to go Jonathan,' I said again, wiping away my tears.

'Please don't do this. Please,' he begged taking a step forward wrapping me in his arms. 'Please Sofia.'

A few weeks before 'the day' March 1983.

Unable to say anymore I looked away from his grief because if I dared to look into those beautiful blue eyes, I would melt and not leave. The truth was I did love him, I adored his every breath, but I had to be sensible and think of Andreas, I had to go back. I needed to explain to him what had happened between Jonathan and me. I owed him that much. There was, however, a small matter I needed to clear up first with my papa; there was the matter of my missing letters. I wanted an explanation.

Jonathan rang me a cab and I left him without an embrace, without a kiss, not even a goodbye. I just left. That was the hardest thing I ever had to do, I felt my heart was wrenched from inside me. I sat in the back of the car and cried all the way to London. Nothing compared to how I was feeling right now, for I knew Jonathan would be watching as the cab drove away, wondering how I could have just left him, how it had gone so horribly wrong. I felt confused - it was all such a mess. My stomach felt like a rock, heavy and dragging, a nauseous feeling had set in and I was sure I would be sick by the time I got to papa's apartment.

My papa had once again managed to do what he did best and that was to play with our lives as if he had a right to do so, just because he was 'papa' and nothing and nobody was too big or that brave to stand in his way. But today I was going to change all of that, I was on my way to see him and I wouldn't be leaving 'til he heard me out, and seeing that he'd already broken all the rules himself the day he cheated on mama, there now were no more lessons he could teach me.

As the cabby approached the security gates, they opened slowly and we were allowed inside the private car park. I got out and asked the driver to keep the meter running as I needed him to take me to the Airport after I'd dealt with my papa. The innocent naive girl that had returned here that afternoon with Christina from Camden Market did not exist anymore. I was not that same Sofia. I kept telling myself I was strong and could confront him, trying to convince myself I had a right to do so. '*I wasn't a child anymore but a woman,*' I kept saying over and over in my head - so many times that I would have no choice but to believe it.

The lift doors opened and as I got in they closed behind me, before I knew it they were open again - I was on the eighth floor and I had to get out. I walked towards his apartment clutching my handbag so tightly to

A few weeks before 'the day' March 1983.

my chest that I could hardly breathe and my hands were sweating so much so that I had to stop to take out a handkerchief to wipe them, but I was shaking and my bag fell from my hands and so did its entire contents, emptying all over the floor. I bent down grabbing at my lipstick and brush and every other useless thing girls have in their handbags. I stood up, brushed myself down and took in a deep breath. I could see the door of his apartment and there was no going back, so I hurriedly made my way to it before I had any chance of changing my mind and for a second I just stood staring, not at the door, but into nothingness - then I rang the bell.

'Sofia?' He said, as he opened the door. He had a surprised look on his face as though he was expecting to see somebody else. 'Sofia, come in,' he moved out of the way.

I entered the apartment a little reluctantly as I looked around me, my eyes suspiciously searching - for what, I wasn't too sure. I had a bad feeling and all of a sudden I knew I'd made a huge mistake coming here.

'Were you expecting someone else papa?' I asked, turning to look his way.

'No of course not my princess,' he said a little tense. 'So how are you?' He took me into his arms, 'where is Andreas?'

'I'm fine papa. Andreas is in Cyprus. It's a bit late in the day for you not to be dressed papa. Are you unwell?' I snarled.

'I'm well. Are you here to choose your wedding dress?' He asked making polite conversation.

'No. No papa my dress is being finished for me in Cyprus as we speak,' I snapped back.

'So why are you here without Andreas? There isn't a problem is there princess?' His tone turned from anxiety to concern.

'Are you sure you're not expecting someone papa?' I ignored his question.

'Are you hungry? What would you like? Or perhaps you prefer we eat out. I hear they do a good 'scabby...'

'I'm not hungry papa,' I replied before he could finish.

'Well let us go out anyway. Let's go for a walk by the river. You like the river,' he begged. 'I'll go and get dressed.'

'Papa I need to speak to you,' I said, putting my hand on his arm. 'Please, sit down.'

138

A few weeks before 'the day' March 1983

But he didn't sit down, he just stood waiting. I didn't know how to begin so I just said it - I asked him, 'I want to know about the letters. Explain to me about my letters papa.'

'You want me to explain about your letters?' He asked, glaring at me in an intimidating way.

'Yes papa I want to know,' I replied, expecting him to have answered in that tone. Surprisingly I was ready for this.

'You do not question me, Sofia. Do you hear?' He frowned. 'I do the questioning.'

'I want to know about my letters papa,' I repeated louder, I wasn't going to feel threatened this time.

'Your letters? Your... letters? You do not question me! I am your papa!' He raised his voice.

'I don't care! They were my letters and you had no right!' I screamed at him. I was shaking uncontrollably. I had never spoken to him in that way before and I had never shouted at him.

'I'm warning you my girl!' He growled.

I could see sheer madness raging in his eyes. 'Don't warn me papa. I'm not a child anymore! Tell me about my letters!' I demanded.

'I took your letters! Yes I took them! Did you think I was going to let whatever you had started continue with that boy?!'

'You took my letters - playing God?! How could you? How dare you? You don't own ME! You think you do but you don't!' I didn't get a chance to say anymore, I felt the force of his hand on my face knocking me as I lost my balance and fell to the sofa.

'But they were addressed to May. How could you have known?' I said quietly, holding my face.

'Did you think I was born yesterday? I told you I would deal with Jonathan Guilbey,' he said standing over me. 'How could you think I didn't know?'

'I NEVER want to see you again,' I sobbed.

I picked my handbag up off the floor and the temptation and force of my anger led me to my next definite move. Without eye contact I made my way towards his bedroom, took hold of the door handle and pushed it open - there she was, waiting naked in his bed, just as I had expected, another of his many mistresses.

'Goodbye papa,' I sighed, letting go of the handle not bothering to

A few weeks before 'the day' March 1983

close the door - there was nothing left to hide.

I just turned around and headed for the front door. 'I do love you,' I said turning back at him; I then walked out of his apartment and out of his life.

March 1983. Epping England.

Chapter Fourteen

It was only a few weeks away from what was supposed to be the happiest day of my life but instead of going back to Cyprus, I returned home to mama. I was in no condition mentally, nor emotionally, to make any decisions and the only person capable of coming anywhere close to healing me was my *yia'ya* Athena: '*This time your yia'ya's special powers would have to work extra hard,*' mama had said. And without wasting further time, she asked Mr Bradshaw to fetch her.

Yia'ya found me clutching Megan and wrapped in Auntie Freda's comfort blanket on my sofa just as I'd done as a little girl. As soon as I saw her I dropped Megan, threw back my blanket and ran straight to her, '*Yia'ya*! My lovely *yia'ya* Athena!' I sobbed.

'Oh Sofia. Let me see you my sweet child,' she examined my face and at once I breathed in the familiar rosy smell of her perfume.

She guided me back to my sofa where we sat. I don't think I'd ever felt this alone before, even with her here I couldn't shake the feeling. I picked up Megan hoping she'd somehow take all the pain away; I wanted her to take me back to that Christmas Day when my cousin Helen had given her to me. The tears just rolled from my face, I was so full of guilt, I'd hurt Jonathan and I was about to hurt Andreas - my papa didn't love me anymore and I didn't have a clue how to right the wrongs.

'Would you like to talk about it?' *Yia'ya* asked.

'I've been so awful *yia'ya*. I shouted at papa, telling him I never wanted to see him again. I've hurt Jonathan and now I must hurt Andreas.'

'Jonathan Guilbey?' She asked confused.

I nodded.

'How on earth could you have hurt Jonathan Guilbey if you weren't even in England?

I turned to her realising this didn't make any sense - she was unaware I was in love with Jonathan and she didn't have a clue about the letters.

March 1983. Epping England.

'Where do I start?' I sighed.

'At the beginning Sofia,' she cradled me.

When I'd finished telling her about Jonathan, and how much we loved one another, about my letters and how papa took me to Cyprus, tricking me and plotting my marriage to Andreas, only then did she understand the significance of what I was going through, and only then did she want to punish my papa.

'What he did to your mama, Sofia, was unforgivable. But this is, well, shameful!' Her voice trembled, she was so angry.

'What shall I do *yia'ya?*'

She took hold of my hand and placed it in hers, and there was a look in her eyes that said she was about to tell me something that was so personal, something she hadn't spoken about for a long time, maybe something she had never spoken about at all, and as she gave my hand a hesitant squeeze, she began:

'Did I ever tell you about my sister Skevoula? Well I tell you she was a beauty. There wasn't a single, eligible man in our village who hadn't asked her to marry him, but her answer would always be no, and do you know why? Because she was in love, she was in love with Christos...Yes Sofia, your *bapou* and he was in love with her.'

I wasn't too sure I wanted or needed to hear anymore.

'My *patera*, she continued, your great-grand papa, at first tried to stop it, but love is love, and the love they felt for one another was much stronger than any man could come between. So, reluctantly he agreed that one day they would be married, and in time they accepted and loved him like a son.

In 1932 a great flood devastated our village and all of our lives were changed over night. It stills feels like it happened only yesterday; I was just fifteen years old and I'll never forget that day 'til I die.

The rain hadn't stopped pouring all night, so much so that we got sent home from school the next morning because the rooms were swamped. I was quite disappointed because, unlike most girls in the village, I loved going to school and dreamt of becoming a teacher myself one day, but as I said, that day changed everything.

It was about six thirty, early evening and it seemed like everyone from Paphos was on that bus returning home. Some coming from work, some coming from shopping and my *mitera*, your great-grandma, she started

142

March 1983. Epping England.

to panic because it was getting late. There was a terrible storm and as the bus went around a bend in the road, the driver lost control and it swerved, losing direction and plunged into the river.

Ten people from our village died that day and my sister Skevoula was one of them. There wasn't one family in the whole village that hadn't lost a loved one. Christos was devastated, his life and all that he had fought for had gone - Skevoula was gone.

Six months passed and he was still living with us as if just by being there she lived on. My *patera* and *mitera* took pity on him, they loved him and they didn't have the heart to ask him to leave, so they did what they thought was the right thing to do and that was to give me to him. I didn't have a say in the matter.

Your *bapou* Christos was a fine man Sofia, I couldn't have wished for a better, more loving husband, but he was my sister's fiancé and that's who he was and that's who he would always be.'

She glanced down at me, her loving tender look turned sad, she smiled at me, 'so, to answer your question Sofia, go with your heart,' she said, wiping the tears from her eyes, tears that had been dormant for years. She kissed my forehead and walked out of my room leaving me speechless and that's when I knew what I had to do - whether I could do it was a different matter!

*   *   *   *   *   *   *   *   *

A week before our wedding I found Andreas sitting on the back porch of our house, our tremendous house that papa had built especially for us to move into as soon as we were married. I slowly crept up behind him not wanting to give him a fright.

Softly I said his name, putting my arms around him.

He swung around jumping to his feet, shocked at the sight of me, hardly believing I was standing there in front of him, 'Sofia! Sofia my love! When did you get back?' His tone was filled with such tremendous joy.

'Just now, I came straight here.'

'But I thought, I thought you…'

'Andreas please sit down we need to talk. Please.'

I sat down close to him but as soon as I looked into his eyes I didn't know where to start. I knew I still loved him and I couldn't think of one single reason why I shouldn't be here, why I shouldn't marry him, it was no fault of his, he had done nothing wrong and that was why this would be so difficult but there was no denying it, I'd been unfaithful and I had to tell him about Jonathan.

'I saw Jonathan Guilbey while I was away,' I began. 'There is no easy way of telling you Andreas.'

'Then do not say anymore.'

'I must. I must because I love you and I must tell you the truth.'

'Will I want to hear it?' He sighed, worried and confused. A knowing look shadowed his face. 'I do not want to lose you Sofia.'

'I don't want to lose you Andreas. I love you so much. You do believe me, don't you? I want to be here with you, I want to marry you but there's Jonathan,' I started to cry.

'I do not care about him. As long as you are here with me that is all that matters.'

'But I do care about him. I still love him. I want to be with you, I really do but I also love him. I love you Andreas, I do, I do,' I wept.

'Then stay here with me forever my love. Here we will grow more in love with every passing day. I will never let you down.'

'But I have already let you down.'

'No you have not, you only think you have. In time you will forget him.'

'But I have let you down Andreas,' I said again and this time he understood what I had meant.

'The day I asked you to marry me, I meant it Sofia, so we will pretend you did not say that.'

'I don't what to pretend anymore, I can't. I have let you down. I love you but I can't marry you, my love.'

'Sofia, it is okay. We can deal with anything if you want to be with me,' he begged.

'But we can't. Don't you see? I love you both but my heart belongs to only one.' In tears I stood walking slowly to the edge of the porch where I stared out into the vastness. Troodos Mountain looked almost a stone's throw away and in the distance I could hear the tiny brass bells rattling their song as they hung on the sheep running by.

'And that one is not me,' he solemnly replied. I felt his arms around

March 1983. Epping England.

me not wanting to accept defeat, 'stay with me tonight Sofia. Please, for one last time?'

He then kissed me tenderly hoping I'd answer '*Yes*.' All I could do was hold on to him with such purity and affection, for there was no hatred or bitterness between us, there couldn't be, because there had been too much love. Here in my arms was the man who had turned the girl into a woman. It would be hard letting him go, but I had to listen to my heart, and my heart told me it belonged to another, it belonged to Jonathan.

I looked desperately into his gaze, then I gave him the answer he wanted to hear, 'I will, I'll stay but only for tonight my love.'

So we sat together on our porch, watching as the magnificent sun disappeared over the horizon, leaving behind it calmness in our minds and a warmth in our hearts, and as the orange-red skies turned into darkened maroons, we fell asleep wrapped in each other's arms 'til the sun returned to welcome yet another beautiful day.

One day, that was all I promised, just one, but one day had turned into two and two into three, 'til five months had past and I was still there. Andreas never talked about marriage, and never again mentioned Jonathan. He just loved me everyday, hoping I'd gradually forget the past and stay here with him forever, and now that we were expecting our first child there could be no looking back. I never needed convincing that what we had was good, I knew Andreas would look after me when I was sick, wipe away my tears when I was sad, and make me laugh when I was feeling down.

I don't think another woman expecting a child had been more spoilt, and the bigger I got, the more protective he became. Until finally that special day had come, November 6th 1983, the day Violet Athena arrived into our world. The joy and the happiness we felt was so overwhelming that we thought our hearts would burst with the love we felt for this little person.

'What a delightful child, an angel, she is beautiful,' said my Auntie Freda, cradling Violet in her arms.

'She looks just like her mama,' smiled Uncle Kosta.

'Yes she does.'

'Let us return her to her cot Sofia. Babies are very cunning and before long she will not let you put her down.'

March 1983. Epping England.

'And God forbid she becomes spoilt like her mama,' teased Andreas.

'Well having a papa like you my love, you will spoil her no doubt!' I laughed, taking Violet from auntie.

'Bring her to me Sofia; I need to kiss my little girl before she goes up to bed.'

I handed her over to him and sat down beside them, watching as he carefully held her in his arms as if she was the most precious thing in the world.

'Thank you,' I said, putting my arm around them both and giving him a kiss.

'No Sofia, thank you my love. She is perfect!'

I smiled, completely understanding the true meaning of unconditional love. Yes, I loved her, I loved her so much and I was so happy, I really was, but Jonathan was never too far from my thoughts. I didn't want him to be, I tried not to let him take over, not to let him spoil what I had with Andreas, but day after day I'd sit on the porch with my canvas and oils thinking back to the time we spent together in Jersey, the night in the summerhouse when we first made love, and how my heart broke, never to be completely mended, the moment I left him.

I hated myself for having these thoughts - these desires, but they wouldn't leave me alone, haunting my dreams. I found myself wanting him more as time went by, wanting to call out his name when making love to Andreas, closing my eyes and imagining it was him I was with. Andreas had hoped that with everyday that passed we would never part and believed that by us having had Violet it was a sign that we should be together. But he also knew that my heart was torn apart and would always belong to Jonathan.

April 17th 1985 my Birthday, Cyprus:

As time went by I wondered how Jonathan's life had turned out and if he still thought about me. I hadn't seen him for two long years and I sometimes imagined him all by himself never having got married, never having loved again. How selfish was I? Did I not think he deserved to be happy? Did he not deserve to be loved?

Of course he deserved to be loved - but only by me. So why had he not come to rescue me - my *'knight in shining armour'*? If he rescued me, then he would be loved!

146

March 1983. Epping England.

I'd heard he'd been living in Jersey for the past six months or so, having inherited Mulberry House after Aunt Vi had left it to him in her will. I'd also heard he'd been finding comfort in the arms of another, his house-keeper - a woman by the name of Emily Thomas.....Mrs Emily Thomas.

I, on the other hand, could only find a small margin of comfort in the knowledge that she was a *Mrs*, hoping he didn't love, nor need her - just want her only for those cold Jersey nights to keep him warm. I tried moving Emily Thomas far from my mind as possible, but even though I hadn't met her, nor had I any wish to, I kept seeing her with him in our psychedelic kitchen, on our beach at the back of the house and even on our hill.

Was she now the lady of the manor? I couldn't bear the thought of them together, her in his arms, in his bed, making love to him everyday. I think I hated her - this Emily Thomas, the woman whose arms he was finding comfort in. Was I never to find peace again? I had some kind of peace before she came along, my own peace and serenity.

Andreas began to witness a new Sofia, a Sofia he hadn't seen before, a Sofia that was uptight, short-tempered and unhappy - becoming distant and withdrawn.

'Is there something bothering you my love?' He asked, wrapping his arms around my shoulders, his hands comfortably finding their way under my dressing gown.

'No,' I shook my head my stare fixed to my canvas.

'I am tired of this silence Sofia.'

Rejecting his advances I pulled away from him as I stood up to get away.

'You have changed Sofia. I feel I do not know you anymore.'

'Nonsense!' I shouted, walking quickly into the house. I thought if I could get away from him I wouldn't have to continue with this conversation because if I stood in front of him any longer I might scream out what I really wanted to say. I wanted to shout out how much I missed Jonathan, how I wanted him everyday, how I was still madly and passionately in love with him and, most of all, how insanely jealous I was of Mrs Emily Thomas!

'Sofia, I am speaking to you!' He shouted back. 'Come back out here!'

'I'm tired Andreas. I'm going to bed.'

March 1983. Epping England.

'Sofia!'

'Goodnight Andreas!'

He ran to catch up with me in our bedroom and I remembered the nights I could hear my mama rowing with papa and I hated it then and I hated this now.

'Sofia, my princess,' he said, taking hold of my arm. 'I do not want us to row. Please.'

'Don't call me your princess. Papa called me that.'

'I do not want us to row. Do you hear?' He said, drawing me closer to him.

'Neither do I, my love,' I replied, my eyes dropped from his stare.

'What is the matter? Please speak to me. Tell me.'

'It's nothing. I've been a fool, a selfish fool.'

'Promise me we will never row again.'

'I promise,' I said, apologetically kissing him.

'Come now, get dressed. Let us go out and celebrate, it is your birthday my love.'

April 17th 1985, that same day. Jersey:

Jonathan had just spent the evening gambling the night away. He had been on a winning streak, and stumbled home only when the casino had finally closed and his winning streak had finally gone, along with all his money. He didn't care - money was not a problem anymore. He'd almost forgotten the days when he was a struggling university student, living at the campus on a tight budget and only making ends meet with help from three other room-mates. Now he was a successful lawyer and the proud owner of Mulberry House.

The spectacular house on Mulberry Hill had been in his family for two hundred years, handed down from generation to generation and now down to him. He was the eldest of Aunt Vi's nieces and nephews, and her favourite, looking upon him as the son she never had, (especially after having been given her beloved Alfred's middle name). He did, however sometimes wonder if this spectacular house would ever hear the sound of laughter again, or whether it would again witness children excitedly running around trying to get ready for a fun day down at the beach...

It must have been gone three a.m, when upon entering the house he was greeted by Betsy, a scruffy little Border Collie he'd bought on a

148

March 1983. Epping England.

whim one rainy afternoon when he'd seen her sleeping in the window of a pet shop in town, and hadn't been able to resist her.

'Hello Betsy girl,' he said, bending down to give her head a friendly pat. 'You hungry? I am.' Betsy wagged her tail jumping up as if to say 'yes' then followed him into the kitchen knowing all too well she was about to be given an early morning feast. She sat waiting, watching while Jonathan poked his head into the larder to see what he could rustle up at such an ungodly hour. When he eventually pulled out a loaf of bread and the jar of onions Aunt Margaret had pickled last Christmas, he went to the refrigerator and took out some ham. 'Pickled onions girl?' He asked, giving the jar a shake in front of poor Betsy's nose, but she gave a disapproving little yelp. 'Maybe not hey? Here have some ham instead, to celebrate her birthday,' he said, dropping a few slices into her bowl. He then carefully piled the ham in-between two thickly cut wedges of bread, making a sandwich that was so unattractive, if Aunt Vi were alive to see it, she would not have cared to entertain in a million years. He carried it into the sitting room with the jar of pickled onions and sat in his favourite armchair by the window over-looking the sea. 'Happy birthday Sofia,' he said, taking a bite. 'Betsy come here girl,' and there they sat in near darkness. The moon shone through the half drawn curtains, glistening over the ocean looking like a luminous dance floor, finally sending them into a deep sleep.

'Jonathan!' Emily called as loudly as she could. 'Jonathan!'

It was midday and Jonathan was still slumped sleeping with Betsy at his feet, both had no intension of waking up. She called and called but he couldn't hear her. So she tried to open the door but the key he'd given her was now jammed in the lock.

'Jonathan!' She called out again 'til she eventually woke Betsy and she began to bark.

'What's up Betsy?' Jonathan grunted, aching from head to toe and struggling to open his eyes. Betsy just carried on barking, running from one room to the next in excitement. She knew someone was at the door and she also knew that someone was Emily.

'Emily?' He frowned, opening the door surprised to see her standing there. 'Emily what are you doing here on a Sunday?'

March 1983. Epping England.

'Well, somebody's happy to see me,' she laughed, bending down to say hello to Betsy. 'I thought you might need some human company,' she continued, looking straight into Betsy's face. 'Anyway I made you a pie, your favourite, apple.'

'Thanks, but you didn't have to.'

'I'll put the kettle on then. Tea?' She said, making her way to the kitchen with Betsy following close behind.

'Emily!'

'Yes Jonathan?' She asked, stopping to look at him.

'Nothing,' he shrugged, 'I'm going to take a shower.'

'Right. Well I'll take Betsy for a run first while you do that.'

'Okay.'

'Come on little girl,' she said. 'Let's go.'

Jonathan stood by the kitchen window watching Emily as she strolled down to the beach. Betsy loved running on the sand and going into the water waiting excitedly for Emily to throw her a stick to fetch - which she did over and over again until they were both exhausted and soaking wet!

By the time they got back Jonathan had showered and left. He'd not asked for Emily's company that day so she would have to entertain herself or leave. After a few hours he returned to a half darkened and empty house with only Betsy - his trusted canine friend - running down the stairs to greet him, waggling her tail as she jumped to welcome him home.

'Hello girl. Has Emily gone home?' He asked, switching on the light in the closet to hang up his coat. 'My God! I look frightful. Don't let me sleep on the armchair tonight, d'you hear me girl?' He said, looking at his reflection in the mirror.

He then patted Betsy on the head and made his way upstairs; and noticing a dimly lit lamp on in his bedroom he quickened his pace and as he swung open the door he saw her, sitting in his bed, naked and making herself available to him. Then without a single word, and not taking his eyes away from hers, she led him to her, though before he even touched her she felt aroused; the mere presence of him had her head spinning and her heart missing beats. Towering over her, she took hold of his hand and kissed it, placing it upon her body, knowing

150

March 1983. Epping England.

what was to come.

Tenderly, he stroked back her long flaming red hair that tussled freely on her slender shoulders, exposing her perfectly rounded breasts, letting out an erotic sigh willing him not to stop. He closed his eyes and allowed his imagination to take him elsewhere. His lips found their way around Emily's warm body, not in a hurry, just taking their time, touching and caressing her. She begged for more, pleading him to make love to her. Yet it wasn't Emily's name whirling around in his head, not Emily's name he wanted to say and he knew his lips need not speak, because his mind was shouting it out anyway. 'Sofia,' he repeated, 'Sofia.'

Summer, July 1985. Cyprus.

Chapter Fifteen

I had just sat down after running around the house not knowing what to do first. I'd laid the table, carved the meat, dressed the salad, sliced the bread, put a thousand garlic cloves into the *zanziki*, hoping they loved garlic filled natural yoghurt, and I uncorked the bottle of wine. Andreas was on his way with my Uncle Kosta, and they were bringing home my family.

Oh my God! My entire family!

My Auntie Freda had helped make the desserts, *trillions* of them; I was so excited! We'd been cooking all week, driving poor Andreas and Uncle Kosta insane, sending them out for groceries every five minutes: '*How much more Sofia?*' Andreas would ask me and each time I would reply: '*Well, there are a lot of us my love.*'

I was so exited about their arrival especially as this was a special occasion. Cousin Helen had agreed to become pen friends with Andreas' brother Manoli and their friendship had blossomed, they had fallen madly in love and were now to be married.

'Sofia! Sofia!' I heard Christina, Irini and Elizabeth calling out my name. I took one look at Auntie Freda, shot up from my chair and started to run.

'They're here auntie. They're here,' I screamed, running so fast I had to kick off my flip flops for fear of tripping over.

I opened the front door and fell into their arms. What a delight! We were jumping for joy! Jumping up and down, crying and laughing, it was so all overwhelming. Then, out of no where, my cousins joined us, Helen and little Anna, Fivo, Christos and Kiri.

'I can't believe you're all here!' I cried.

'It's been a long time!' Yelled Helen.

'We've missed you so much!' Kiri shrieked.

'You're looking old cousin! You're looking great cousin!' Bellows of voices were surrounding me I couldn't quiet make out who was asking, except for when Fivo laughed demanding to know, 'Where's the food?'

Everyone roared with laugher and I wanted to hold onto them all - we were kids, all kids once again!

Helen and Manoli's big day soon came around and Helen looked beautiful! I don't think I'd ever seen a more beautiful bride. Manoli took hold of her hand as they stepped out of St Johns church in *Totou* as man and wife!

The crowd exclaimed with happiness as they watched Manoli pick her up into his arms and kiss her. He was such a joker!

He then carefully sat her into the waiting car and they were whizzed off!

When we got to the beach where the reception was being held I stood mesmerized, there hadn't been a single detail overlooked. Arranged under white canopies laced with colourful lanterns the dance floor was lined with tiny spot-lights and tables were covered with crisp white linen showered with an array of beautiful red flowers. The man-made décor mixed with nature set a hypnotic scene.

The happy couple took to the floor for their first formal dance and the crowd once again roared and cheered as Manoli took Helen into his arms.

'Everybody, I give you your bride and groom, the beautiful Helen, and the not so beautiful, Manoli - Mr and Mrs Angelou,' announced the wedding singer to laughter and applause. 'We'd like to see you all join them on the dance floor.'

I looked over to where Andreas was standing holding Violet in his arms talking with his brother Stavros, he excused himself and started walking my way, I felt a sudden discontentment and sadness deep in my heart.

'And *I* would love to dance with my two beautiful girls,' he said stretching out his hand for me to take. He led us both onto the dance floor, holding me so tight for fear I might disappear if he let me go.

'I love you,' he whispered to me.

'I know,' I replied, giving Violet a kiss on her cheek then turning my head to him so he could look into my eyes I said, 'and I love you, my love.' It's what he wanted to hear.

153

Summer, July 1985. Cyprus.

'Good,' he said, wrapping his arm around us both. 'They look so happy.'

'Yes, they do,' I said, turning to look at Helen. She looked absolutely radiant, there was a glow surrounding her - she shone!

'Can I cut in?' Manoli asked taking hold of my waist.

'Be my guest brother but only if I can dance with your gorgeous bride?' Andreas teased, kissing Helen's hand.

'Oh how romantic. Have I just married the wrong brother?' She laughed.

'I think you may have my love,' Manoli joked swinging me around, taking me into the middle of the dance floor.

Everybody parted like the red sea and as the band changed into an up beat rock n' roll tempo, Manoli went in full swing doing the twist! He loved it, and was good too! I tried keeping up with him, he was twisting one way and I twisting the other as we threw our hands in the air. The faster the music went, the quicker we twisted 'til I exhaustedly dropped into his arms and we began to laugh.

'Wow! You were amazing. I could not take my eyes off of you,' said Andreas.

'Don't embarrass me,' I said, with a huge satisfied grin on my face as I tried to catch my breath.

'You loved it out there and I tell you this, I loved watching you.'

'Well, I suppose it was fun. He's great!' I said, 'and he makes my cousin very happy.'

'We could have this Sofia. We can have it all.'

'But we do have it all.'

'Not all Sofia. Let us get married? Can you not see we are meant to be?' Then suddenly he went down on one knee in the middle of the dance floor, 'I have asked you before and I am asking you again, Sofia Constantine, will you make me a happy man? Will you marry me?'

I looked at Andreas, then at Violet, 'yes!' I said, determined to make a go of it this time. He quickly got up off his knee and ran over to where the band was playing, grabbed hold of the microphone and announced it to everyone!

'I have some good news! I have just asked that incredible woman over there to marry me; and she has said yes!' He shouted.

Applause echoed amongst the crowd.

Summer, July 1985. Cyprus.

'Oh, my sweet girl!' Mama cried. 'I'm so very happy for you. Andreas is a good man and he loves you Sofia. He loves you so much. I know he will make you happy my child.'

Summer, July 1985, Jersey:

'Hello,' said a young lad standing at the front door. 'I've come for Sarah.'

'And who are you dear?' Grandma Guilbey asked.

'Who is it grandma?' Jonathan called out.

'I'm Kenny,' he said.

'It's a handsome young man at the door. He says his name is....What is it again dear?'

'Kenny.'

'It's okay Betsy!' Jonathan said holding her back as she barked and scrambled for the door. 'Calm down girl, can I help you?' He asked.

'Yeah, I'm Kenny. I've come for Sarah.'

'And you know Sarah? How?'

Kenny hesitated, not quite sure how to take this interrogation, 'we met when she was here in the summer.'

'Okay Kenny it's like this, Sarah may be a little busy right now so I think its best you return another day.'

'Jonathan!' Sarah called out, running down the stairs. 'It's okay, hi Kenny,' she said. 'He used to feed Mittens when Aunt Vi was not well and in hospital,' she stated.

'Oh, of course, Kenny! You're Kenny? Why didn't you say?'

But Kenny was a little nervous of Jonathan and he saw Betsy wasn't very thrilled either, so he didn't reply.

'Look there is nothing to be afraid of. Just make sure you bring Sarah home by five. Okay?' He smirked.

'Jonathan!' She tutted. 'Come on Kenny let's go.'

Through half open windows, the warm evening breeze entered the dining room to the caressing sound of gentle waves from the shore. The scented candles flickered softly in china candelabras giving a mystic glow as they released a wonderful aromatic smell of lavender.

'Emily the meal was wonderful,' Henry interrupted the tranquil mood.

'Thank you Mr Guilbey.'

Summer, July 1985. Cyprus.

Grandma Guilbey didn't look up; she just nodded in agreement, still tucking into the last piece of her fish.

'Yes lovey it was. Let me help you clear the dishes,' Margaret said, giving her a friendly smile.

'Are you sure Mrs Guilbey?' asked Emily. 'I can manage.'

'Two pairs of hands are better than one lovey.'

'What did you say Margaret?' Grandma Guilbey butted in.

'Not anything for you to worry about grandma, just asking who wants tea?'

'Ooh! Yes please,' she beamed excitedly.

'I'll get the dessert then,' Emily said, glancing at Jonathan with a grin. '*You like dessert*,' she insinuated, and left the room.

'Well how have you been son?' Asked Henry.

'Good dad.'

'And work?'

'Work's good!'

'Jonathan, are you and that girl?' his eyes twitched towards the kitchen. 'Be careful son, she's married.'

'I know dad. I've got it all under control.'

'Just be careful,' he said again swigging his brandy.

'Another?' Asked Jonathan, raising the decanter to pour one for himself.

'Yes okay, just one more,' he jested. 'What about Sofia?'

'What about her? The last time I saw her was at Aunt Vi's funeral,' he lied, though the mere thought of her brought an image of them in the summerhouse together. He lit his cigar and then offered one to Henry.

'Thanks,' he said taking one. 'I thought you had something special there with that fantastic girl son.'

'So did I. We were both wrong,' he sighed striking a match.

'Problem is son, do you love her?' He said, taking in a drag.

'That was a long time ago dad.'

'That doesn't answer my question now does it?' Henry replied, blowing out a puff of smoke.

Jonathan stood up and walked over to the window and taking hold of the curtain pulled it back to unleash the past - he could see a little fire smouldering on the beach and he heard Sofia's laughter in his ears, he pulled her to him and they kissed. Then as he licked his lips, he

156

Summer, July 1985. Cyprus.

could still taste the sweetness of sugar in his mouth.

'Yes I do still love her dad,' he said, letting go of the curtain.

'It's a little quiet in here. What are you boys talking about?' Asked Margaret, re-entering the room with a tray of overflowing mugs of Earl Grey.

'Ooh tea! I'll have the mug with the pink roses please Margaret,' said grandma, pointing her chubby finger at it.

'The pink roses it is, grandma,' she said, placing it in front of her. 'Jonathan, lovey?'

'Any one mum,' he smirked taking a mug.

'That leaves the blue pansies for you lovey,' she teased, handing the mug over to Henry.

Emily put the large glass dessert bowl on the dining table and began to spoon out the jelly trifle into smaller dishes. 'Goodnight everyone. I'll be in the library if you need me,' she said, glancing over at Jonathan before dismissing herself.

They sat talking for a few hours more, the first to retire was Grandma Guilbey, then Margaret, Henry finally turned in at midnight leaving Jonathan alone to gather his thoughts until Sarah eventually strolled home exhausted.

'What time do you call this?' Jonathan said, so quietly it was almost a whisper.

He was sitting in his favourite armchair with Betsy loyally at his feet.

'Oh my God!' Exclaimed Sarah, half jumping out of her skin with fright. 'Jonathan! What are you doing up?'

'I could ask you the same question.' She said, slumping on the sofa opposite him shattered, just about managing to pat her knee for Betsy to jump up.

'You look worn out,' he continued. 'What have you been up to, I hope you've been behaving?'

'Hello girl,' she said ruffling Betsy's fur as she jumped up on her lap. 'So would you be worn out if you had gone on every single ride at the fair.'

'How well do you know that boy?'

'Kenny? Well enough.' She put Betsy down on the floor and got up to kiss him. 'Give me a hug, I'm off to bed, are you coming up?'

'Soon. Goodnight Sarah. Come on girl,' he said to Betsy and

157

Summer, July 1985. Cyprus.

together they walked to the kitchen. He made some coffee and headed to the beach. Emily stood by the window in the library watching him as he sat on the sand clutching his cup. Inhaling in the last puff from his cigar he stubbed it out into the sand and looked up at the sky. The moon was so bright and stars so brilliant that together they were dazzling to the naked eye. He then pushed his hand into the sand where the warm fine crystals ran through his fingers and felt like golden sugar waiting to be tasted. As Emily pressed her face closer to the window she was fully aware who he was thinking of, knowing that he yearned to taste the sugar on Sofia's lips, the sugar that had been so sweet. She also knew there was nothing she could do to help him; Lord only knows how she'd tried. For she wasn't the one he desired, nor who had become his obsession, an addiction he would only stop craving when his longings and desires were complete.

Summer, August 1985, Cyprus:

It had been a truly unforgettable start to the summer. Helen had married Manoli in the most memorable of weddings, and I hoped she would be blissfully content with her life now that she'd married her 'prince' and that they would live their own happy ever after.

Happy ever after - if there was such a thing, because there were no unhappy Greek princesses, were there? – A sceptical myth as my mama was 'living proof' that there were, at least one broken hearted.

It was now time for me to get on with my life. The crazy longings I had for Jonathan would have to stop, be put to one side and locked away, never to be set free again. I'd finally accepted that my *knight in shining armour* would never be coming to rescue me, so I prayed he would leave me alone, because I wanted my own happy ever after...

I laid on a beach towel with Irini, soaking up the Cyprus sun watching Christina splashing Elizabeth as she tried walking gracefully into the sea under the watchful eye of some boys. She was almost twelve, and almost a woman! And it reminded me of the day I first set eyes on Andreas when he had rudely interrupted me.

'Do you think I'll ever meet the right man?' Asked Irini, handing me the suntan lotion to put on her back.

'Yes, of course. Why do you ask that?'

158

Summer, July 1985. Cyprus.

'Just wondering. Didn't you ever wonder?'

'Yes,' I replied, rubbing the lotion in carefully.

'Try not to get it on my costume,' she strictly pointed out. 'How do you know when he's the right one?' She continued. 'How did you know?'

'I suppose you just do.'

'Like you knew it was Andreas?'

'I guess, that's why I'm marrying him before he comes to his senses and changes his mind,' I replied, tightening the lid and handing the bottle back to her.

'I don't think I'll ever know,' she said assumingly, looking over at Elizabeth.

'Not every man is papa, Irini,' I said answering her silent thoughts.

'And not every man is Jonathan,' she said answering mine.

'Please don't mention Jonathan,' I sighed wondering why she had.

'Why? And why are you lying to yourself?'

'*I'm not lying! Lying about what?*' I could hear myself saying as I began to shake.

'I know about Jonathan. I'm sorry but I over heard you telling *yia'ya* Athena.'

'Well you heard wrong, it's over now! I'm sorry, but I don't what to speak about him please.'

'It's not over!'

'Trust me. He doesn't love me anymore,' I said taking a deep breath getting up off the towel.

'I can't believe that! I won't believe it!'

'Where is he then? Is he here?...No!' I snapped looking down at her. 'If he really loved me, why did he let me go? Why didn't he stop me from leaving him?!' I broke down and anxious tears streamed down my face.

'Okay! He didn't stop you Sofia and he's not here but you're not there with him either!' She said, reasoning with my anger.

'Well it would've helped Irini, don't you think?' I gave a little sniff; I needed to get away from talking about Jonathan Guilbey. 'I'm getting an ice cream. Are you coming?' I asked.

'No it's too hot to get up,' she replied, putting on her sunglasses and closing her eyes. She'd said all she had to say.

'I'll bring you one back then.' I ran over the burning sand and across

159

Summer, July 1985. Cyprus.

the road to Mr Roussi's café. As soon as he saw me he welcomed me with a hearty smile and a kiss on the cheek.

'*Yasou* Mr Roussi,' I said, dragging a small iron chair into the shade.

'*Yasou* Sofia.'

I didn't need to remind him anymore, he knew what I was having.

'*Pa'yoto?*' He asked.

'*Para'galo*,' I nodded.

'Right away,' he laughed, digging into the tub for the first enormous scoop!

Chocolate and walnut ice cream! *Lovely*! I thought. 'There you are,' he said, placing an overflowing dish on the table accompanied with a glass of ice cold water.

'Thank you. This is fantastic Mr Roussi.' I tucked into it straight away before it began to melt.

'I glad I make you happy with my *pa'yoto* Sofia,' he replied, in a broad Cypriot accent, taking great satisfaction watching me as I dug in. 'How is Andreas?'

'He's lovely thanks.'

'Tell him I waiting to beat him at backgammon,' he chuckled to himself with the thought of defeating Andreas again.

'Okay Mr Roussi, I will.'

We first met Mr Roussi when Andreas noticed a sign saying he served chocolate and walnut ice cream; '*The best on the island*,' he'd told us.

'There is only one way to find out,' Andreas had replied ordering the largest scoop for me to try.

I had no choice but to indulge, slowly eating the lot while they watched and waited for my verdict. When I had finished, I put done my spoon, swallowed the last mouthful and smiled. There was no more to be said, the judgment was in my smile.

From that day, I had made a new friend and Andreas had met his match. Night after night I would tuck into my ice cream, while he and Mr Roussi battled it out to become 'backgammon champion of the world!'

I suddenly remembered Irini and gulped down the rest of my dish, ordered three little tubs and quickly ran back to the beach before they

160

began to melt.

'*Yasou* Mr Roussi!' I called out to him.

'*Yasou* Sofia!'

I ran across the road and onto the burning sand but as I got closer to where I'd left Irini, I noticed Uncle Kosta standing with her; he was saying something and throwing his arms in the air. I quickly rushed over to them suddenly becoming unnerved and afraid as to why he was acting so peculiar. When Irini saw me her face turned grim and she had a blank stare in her eyes and I knew, there and then, I knew something awful must have happened; 'Oh God! Please don't let it be Violet!' I cried out.

'Christina! Elizabeth!' Irini called for them to get out of the sea. Then she looked over at me and said, 'you must sit down Sofia.'

'It's not my Violet is it? What's happened? Is it papa!? Is it Andreas!? I screamed, so many questions running through my head.

'It's neither Violet nor Andreas,' she reassured me, then taking hold of my arm, she mouthed, 'It's papa.'

'What's happened?! What's happened Irini?! Tell me!' I howled, but she was speechless.

'I'm sorry Sofia there's been an accident...He's gone...He's gone my child,' Uncle Kosta eventually said, his voice so dreary... so dull.

I gave out an enormous scream and suddenly there was no air and I couldn't breath. I felt the blood rush to my head. The ice cream dropped from my hands as I collapsed to the ground.

A Funeral...1985.

Chapter Sixteen

It was the most beautiful day, no different from any other beautiful day in August. I looked up but I had never seen it before, not like this, the sky was powder blue.

'As blue as his eyes,' I heard myself whisper.

I wondered how far up it all went, how deep? If I reached hard enough could I touch that one little cloud up there all alone? I was as invisible as a ghost was. A part of me had stopped living the day he died, a piece was missing.

'Sofia?' I heard Christina say. 'Sofia?'

Just as I was about to touch my cloud in the sky, her voice pulled me back, back to where I didn't want to be. I turned to look at her and for a moment forgot where I was and why; for that single moment I didn't have to face this reality - because my reality was somewhere else.

'It's your turn Sofia,' she said, her voice sounding cheerless and empty as she handed me a white rose.

I reached out to take it from her and the dazzling sun shone upon the crystal butterfly hanging from my bracelet, making it sparkle like a rare diamond, and that's when I saw its' wings flicker as it came back to life.

I put the rose up to my face but even its velvety petals seemed to turn poignant to my touch.

Yes, it was my turn, I thought and I closed my eyes......

When I opened them, I found myself back in England, back from where it had all happened, and a sad, hollow feeling came over me. I looked down at my rose, reminding me it was time to let go, time to say my goodbyes. I'd felt every emotion it was possible to feel; every heartache, every pain, every joy and every laughter, but what I was feeling right now didn't have a name, nothing could compare. I stared down, down to where he was lying, all alone, and as the tears left my eyes, I let my rose drop silently from my hold, watching as it fell to where he was waiting and as it dropped two beautiful white doves were set free.

'Goodbye….goodbye my papa, my friend,' I whispered, only for him to hear.

There was stillness in my soul that felt so inert I thought I might never recover from losing papa. My papa, who had been my hero, my rock. I wanted him back; I hated him for having left me. Whose princess would I be now that he was gone? I locked myself away in my own safe world, not coming out for days. He'd once told me we were invincible: *'Strong like the Gods that watched over us,'* he'd said. But his strength would become our weakness, he was strong and we were weak, that's what he led us to believe and that was the only way he could survive. Only when I'd lost him, could I come to terms with what I'd allowed him to do to me, making me feel guilty for wanting to live my life as Sofia. All I ever wanted was for him to be proud, and to love me unconditionally, love me for who I was, but now it was too late. I would never see him again and he would never meet Violet. She was so much like him, strong willed and full of humour, even at such a tender age; she was strong willed like him yet free spirited like me. *'You're a Constantine through and through,'* I would tell her and she would laugh quietly to herself as if she knew what I meant.

We spent hours together in my room, examining old photo albums. I would explain and she would patiently listen as I told her how great her *bapou* was and how much he would have loved her if he were alive.

Page after page, every picture told a different story:

'Do you know who this baby is?' I asked her, turning the first page.

'No mama,' she replied, looking up at me adoringly, staring into my eyes for the answer.

'It's your mama; it's me when your *yia'ya* Elena first brought me home from the hospital. I was just one week old.'

1962:

'She's beautiful, just perfect!' I remember papa telling me of that day…He said it with such delight, over and over as if nobody had heard him the first time.

'She's absolutely gorgeous!' he kept saying.

'Yes, and to think you didn't want her, you wanted a boy,' bapou Christos

teasingly reminded him.

'Have you seen her eyes? Take a look at her beautiful blue-eyes and she has blonde hair. Can you believe it?' Papa continued, completely disregarding bapou's comments.

'Well you wanted to name your son Pedri. Now what will you call her?

'Sofia. We will call her Sofia,' he said, cradling me in his arms.

'Let's turn the page,' I said, smiling down at Violet.

Her little hands stopped at a picture of me with the biggest smile and a front tooth missing. I was sitting with Irini and mama under the willow tree in our garden a few days after we'd moved into Holly Blue. I was two years old.

1964:

That was the day Uncle Mike came over. Still at university and a young struggling photographer, he was free and single and yet to meet Aunt Demi. His assignment was, 'The Family.'

'Put on their best frocks,' he'd told mama.

I remembered how he kept asking me to smile because he was finding it quite amusing - me having a missing front tooth.

'Don't worry Sofia, you're still beautiful,' he kept saying. 'Next time try not going over the handle bars.'

'Oh, stop teasing her Mike,' mama smiled with a slight giggle, trying not to laugh. 'It's bad enough Harry has given back the tricycle to dear Margaret.'

'That was a bit harsh. Don't you think?' Uncle Mike replied.

'Yes, but you know Harry and his princesses. Now all bikes are banned!'

'That was a funny picture of mama, wasn't it?' I said, looking down at my missing tooth, and she nodded.

'Turn the page mama?'

'Okay.'

'Look!' she said, her little fingers were pointing.

'Oh my God!' I laughed, 'Yes, look Violet! That's your Aunties, Irini and Christina. Oh and there's Paris and Desy and mama's best friend, Aunt May, and Martin Berry and there's, Keith... Keith Barton,' I said and then I stopped...

A Funeral...1985.

Keith Barton was such a lad! Always in the middle of every game - if we were playing it, then he would be there! His favourite of course was 'kiss chase' and he ALWAYS chased me! I would run as fast as I could but he would always catch me. Papa would have gone crazy if he'd ever found out!

Oh, Keith Barton how could I forget? When at only six years old, he'd asked his mum to drop him off at our house, barely able to reach the door bell, he'd come to ask if I could 'come out to play.'

When papa answered the door, he looked down and asked what he wanted; 'Yes. Can I help you little boy, what do you want?' He smiled.

'I've come to play with Sofia,' said Keith, sporting a huge grin that went right across his face.

My papa's face suddenly dropped, and his smile disappeared; 'No!' He replied. 'Sofia cannot come out to play. She is busy!'

Yes I was busy!... Doing what? I wasn't too sure, a papa kind of busy.

'My name is Keith and I've come to play with Sofia,' he said again, refusing to leave.

'Well Keith, I'm sorry. As I said, she's very busy. Now you run along boy!'

'That's a funny little horse mama,' said Violet, giggling. 'Look! *Bapou's* got a floppy hat on!'

1969:

Seven years old, Southend and a pony called Jack!

All the parents watched as the assistants took their children for a walk on the beach, each one sitting on a small pony, going round and round in a huge circle. Five ponies, five children, and five assistants! Oh! And MY papa and his floppy hat! My papa was so petrified I would fall off; he insisted he would hold my pony's reins and go around with us so there we were, four ponies, four children, me, my papa and his floppy hat, the assistant and Jack! It was quite embarrassing at the time but looking back at the photo I guess that was just my papa - how amusing.

'Your *bapou* could be so funny sometimes,' I laughed, staring down at the photo.

'You're sitting on Jack, mama, and *bapou's* wearing a floppy hat,' she giggled, putting her tiny hands up to her face.

'Yes I am.'

Then, she put her nose right up to him, making sure she got a closer look and she kissed him.

'Love you *bapou*,' she said kissing the photo, over and over. 'Love you.'

'Oh Violet, you make mama so very sad, but happy too when you do that,' I told her. I didn't want to turn anymore pages. 'Now mind your little fingers my darling, we've seen enough for today,' I sighed.

Just as we closed the album, a picture fell out and landed by my feet. I picked it up carefully turning it around - it took my breath away. It was the one of all my family on the 5th of November, 1976...Guy Fawkes night around *yia'ya's*. It was the picture that Uncle Mike took when everyone was happy and ignorance was bliss! '*Come on everybody say cheese*,' his words echoed in my ears, '*haloumi*,' we shouted! *I didn't find that funny anymore*.

'Come on Violet my darling, let's go downstairs,' I said, slipping the picture randomly back into the book.

There was something I needed to do, something very important. I took Violet to the conservatory where I knew I would find one of my sisters - I needed to be alone. I found Elizabeth, 'Elizabeth, can you watch over Violet? I have something I must do,' I asked.

'Yes, of course, it would be a pleasure,' she said tickling her as she picked her up. 'Are you hungry? Shall we have some *baklava* and milk?' Elizabeth asked, planting a kiss on her rosy little cheeks.

I ran back up to my bedroom, got out my box of writing paper and sat on my sofa with Auntie Freda's blanket. '*Wrap it around you and I will be there, keeping you warm like the Cyprus sun*,' I could hear her saying and if there was one time I needed her here, it was now! I put my pen to paper and began:

Saturday, 24thAugust 1985

My dearest Andreas,

It's been three weeks since I left you, three weeks but it feels like a life-time. I

166

A Funeral...1985.

know I've promised you everyday that I will be with you soon, but it's not been that easy leaving mama and my sisters, they've needed me, and I've needed them too. The truth is I suppose this is where I belong. I love you so much Andreas, you will never know how much, but I'm sorry I won't be returning to Cyprus. I have, as I think you know, lived my life for someone other than for me, and I think you also know who that someone was ...my papa!

Now it's my turn Andreas, but this is so heart-breaking because I do love you, I know that is hard to believe but I do. I will always cherish the times we had together and I will smile whenever I remember you, and how special Troodos Mountain was to us. Please don't hate me, but if I don't do it now, I never will and I will forever live in his shadow.

Please just try to understand, I'm not doing this only for me but for Violet, I cannot live a lie anymore...She deserves to know the truth. I'm so very sorry.

I love you now and always will,

Sofia xxxxx

I folded the letter then quickly putting it into the envelope ran out of my room and headed downstairs to find Mr Bradshaw.

'Mrs Bradshaw,' I said, passing her by in the hallway. She was carrying some linen towards mama's bedroom. 'Have you seen Mr Bradshaw?'

'Yes Miss Sofia, he's in the garage cleaning the Bentley. Do you need him? Shall I fetch him for you?'

'No, it's okay. Thank you, I'll go and find him.'

'As you wish Miss,' she smiled.

She then turned and continued on her way.

When I got to the hall, the grandfather clock struck its chimes and I quickly hurried past it heading for the back garden where I found Mr Bradshaw waxing the car Papa's beloved Bentley!

'Hello Mr Bradshaw.'

'Oh, good afternoon Miss Sofia,' he said, stopping to look up at me.

'Papa loved this car,' I remembered, as I gently stroked the bonnet.

'Yes he did, it was his *'baby.'* She is a beauty. Don't you think?'

'Yes, she is,' I replied, my mind going back to all the fantastic drives we went on through the forest. 'Mr Bradshaw can you post this letter for me please. It's very important you catch the last post.'

A Funeral...1985.

'No problem Miss Sofia I'll do it right away,' he said adding quite unexpectedly. 'We do miss your papa terribly'. I think he must have felt what I was thinking.

'Sorry Miss Sofia, It's not my place.'

'No, it's okay Mr Bradshaw. Thank you for your kindness.'

'I'll go now,' he smiled, looking down at my letter.

Mr Bradshaw was a good soul, and he had always been kind to us and he had admired my papa. It was nice to have him and Mrs Bradshaw here; along with Lynsey they made it all so very homely still. 'Oh and can you also pick up these tickets for me?' I asked, giving him the piece of paper that I'd written on.

'Yes Miss Sofia. Going somewhere?' He asked, managing a smile.

'Yes.' I nodded. 'Home, I'm going home Mr Bradshaw.'

Saturday, 31st August 1985:

This was it, what I'd dreamt about all my life. I had finally come to my senses; I was eventually doing things my way, for me and only me! I held on to Violet's tiny hand and she held onto Megan's as we went through passport control and as I took one last look back at mama and my sisters, *yia'ya* Athena smiled at me, she knew my heart was leading me this time.

'I love you,' she read my lips as I whispered and 'I love you more,' she replied.

I wiped my tears and left. *That* was the most thrilling, yet scariest feeling I had ever felt.

We boarded the tiny plane and I sat down next to Violet fastening her safety belt, I caught sight of the pretty hostess, 'would you like a blanket Miss?' She asked.

'No, we're fine thanks,' and as soon as I closed my eyes, the plane took off. Half an hour later we were in the arrivals lounge and I was calling Peter:

'Hello,' I said as soon as he answered.

'Hello. Who's this?'

'It's Sofia! Sofia Constantine! Do you remember me?!' I was shouting as if I were my mama on the phone to Auntie Freda in Cyprus.

'Sofia? Sofia how are you luv?' He said, his voice sounding genuinely

A Funeral...1985.

pleased. 'Where are you?'

'I'm at the airport here in Jersey. Are you free Peter? Can you come and collect us?'

'Yes of course I can Sofia. I'll be there in fifteen minutes luv.'

'Thanks Peter, we'll be outside,' I said, hanging up.

Within fifteen minutes and as promised, Peter was at the airport.

'Violet, I'd like you to meet Peter,' I told her. 'This is my very special friend.'

'Hello Peter,' she said.

'Hello Violet. Who's that you've got there?'

'Megan,' she smiled.

'Hello Megan,' he smiled back, and gave Violet a friendly hand shake. Then he looked up at me. 'How are you luv?' He said, taking my case.

'I'm fine Peter.'

'Where to luv? Mulberry House?'

'How did you guess?' I nodded.

He opened the door helping us in and we were off. The butterflies were now beginning to dance in my stomach once again and the nearer we got, the faster they were dancing! I felt some kind of magic happening to me and I couldn't wait, I couldn't wait anymore!

'Peter?' I called out.

'Yes luv? We're not going back are we?'

'No! Could you go a little faster please?!'

'Done!' he said, putting his foot down on the accelerator, so rapidly that I thought we were going to fly.

'Peter?!'

'Yes?'

'Umm, not *that* fast,' I smirked.

I sat with Violet staring excitedly out of the window as Peter drove us along the coast and to my delight there it was again, the Queen Elizabeth Castle. Oh how perfectly romantic it all felt - Peter taking me to my *knight*. I took in a deep breath and automatically I smelt the sugared doughnuts that took my senses back, back to the nights I spent here with Jonathan on the beach and I started to cry.

When we turned into the narrow street where the houses were all joined together, I knew it would not be too long before I saw him.

A Funeral...1985.

Then all at once I looked up and there it was, Mulberry House, as elegant as ever. Peter stopped the car and waited for my indication to get out.

'Will you be alright luv?' He asked seeing the anticipation on my face.

I nodded but no words would come out, I couldn't speak. I just took hold of Violet's hand and we walked slowly towards the house. The thought of Andreas sitting on the porch holding my letter flashed momentarily in my mind.

I opened the small side gate and we went down the narrow sandy pathway that led to the beach. With a further intake of my breath, I recognised the familiar smell of the sea and I could see the seagulls as they flew skimming the waters surface, searching for their daily feast.

Andreas read until there were no more words, only tears, and as the tears fell from his eyes, they fell from mine too...

Then I saw Jonathan, just as I remembered him, he was sitting alone on a bench at the back of the house looking out at the ocean. I whispered to Violet and as I let go of her and she ran straight to him. Betsy wagged her tail as she sniffed Violet's tiny hand, who'd began to giggle.

'Hello,' he said, looking over at her. 'And who are you?'

'Violet and this is Megan,' she replied, holding her up to show him.

'I'm Jonathan, and this is Betsy,' he laughed as Betsy licked Violet's hand.

'She likes you Violet, where's your mummy?'

'My mama is over there,' she said fussing Betsy.

'You said Megan?' He paused, realising what Violet had said.

'Yes,' she nodded, 'she was my mama's.'

Jonathan turned his head slowly to look behind and when he saw me walking towards him...he knew!

'Sofia?... Sofia is it really you?' He was calling as he ran to me. He lifted me up into his arms. 'Sofia! Sofia please tell me its true; tell me I'm not dreaming. Tell me you've come back and you'll never leave me again,' he was crying, as he spun me round and round.

'Oh Jonathan! Jonathan I never left you. I never left you my love!' I cried.

A Funeral…1985.

When he finally put me down, I took hold of his hand and led him to his daughter. 'Violet,' I said. 'Come and meet your papa my darling.'

She ran to him so naturally it took his breath away. Yet, to her he was no stranger as I had shown her pictures and explained as best as I could on our short journey here all about her real papa.

He lifted her up and kissed her, instantly loving her every breath. I knew this was the unconditional love *I'd* been searching for, as he was looking at her as he had forever looked at me.

I'd finally found my *Happy Ever After*… and I was never letting it go!

The End